Select Praise for

Andrew Krivak

"Some writers are good at drawing a literary curtain over reality, and then there are writers who raise the veil and lead us to see for the first time. Krivak belongs to the latter."
—National Book Award judges' citation

"[Krivak's] work has been compared to William Faulkner's in its rich sense of place, to Wendell Berry's in its attentiveness to natural beauty, and to Cormac McCarthy's in its deep investigation of violence and myth. Yet all of Krivak's writing, and especially his fiction, presents a truly singular vision."
—Anthony Domestico, *Image*

"An extraordinarily elegant writer, with a deep awareness of the natural world."
—Roxana Robinson, *New York Times Book Review*

"Eloquent, sensitive."
—Jennifer Haigh, *Boston Globe*

"Delivers revelation after revelation."
—Ben Fountain

"Incandescent." **—Marlon James**

"Spare and lovely." **—Adam Johnson**

"Grand and unforgettable." **—Maaza Mengiste**

"A writer of rare and powerful elegance."
—Mary Doria Russell

"[A] singular talent." **—Jesmyn Ward**

Mule Boy

The Books of the Dardan Trilogy

Like the Appearance of Horses

The Signal Flame

The Sojourn

Also by Andrew Krivak

The Bear (fiction)

A Long Retreat: In Search of a Religious Life (nonfiction)

Ghosts of the Monadnock Wolves (poetry)

Islands (poetry)

Mule Boy

Andrew Krivak

Bellevue Literary Press
New York

First published in the United States in 2026
by Bellevue Literary Press, New York

For information, contact:
Bellevue Literary Press
90 Broad Street
Suite 2100
New York, NY 10004
www.blpress.org

This is a work of fiction. Characters, organizations, events, and places (even those that are actual) are either products of the author's imagination or are used fictitiously.

Library of Congress Cataloging-in-Publication Data
Names: Krivak, Andrew, author.
Title: Mule boy / Andrew Krivak.
Description: First edition. | New York : Bellevue Literary Press, 2026.
Identifiers: LCCN 2025006983 | ISBN 9781954276468 (paperback ; acid-free paper) | ISBN 9781954276475 (ebook)
Subjects: LCGFT: Novels.
Classification: LCC PS3561.R569 M85 2026 | DDC 813/.54--dc23/eng/20250214
LC record available at https://lccn.loc.gov/2025006983

Bellevue Literary Press would like to thank all its generous donors—individuals and foundations—for their support.

This publication is made possible by the New York State Council on the Arts with the support of the Office of the Governor and the New York State Legislature.

Book design and composition by Mulberry Tree Press, Inc.

Bellevue Literary Press is committed to ecological stewardship in our book production practices, working to reduce our impact on the natural environment.

♾ This book is printed on acid-free paper.

Manufactured in the United States of America.

10 9 8 7 6 5 4 3 2

paperback ISBN: 978-1-954276-46-8
ebook ISBN: 978-1-954276-47-5

For John George Kriváк,
and for Anna and her children,
who waited for him

To the roots of the mountains I went down —
the underworld's bolts against me forever

—Jonah 2:7

I

AND ON THAT DAY HE WALKED THE DIRT ROAD from the patch past the colliery toward the entrance of the shaft, the only light visible coming from the breaker with its multitude of filament bulbs inside and outside and along each apparatus that drove it shining brighter than any constellation any man or boy who labored within, around, or below that breaker would ever see, and he could hear it, alive and throbbing with its steady heartbeat throb that pounded away while he slept, pounded away when he woke, pounded away the length of every day there was work in that mine, he even remembering as a boy, sick in bed in the clapboard patch house and gazing out the window at the behemoth, asking his mother if it would ever stop, and without turning to look at the structure that hulked there lit and monstrous against the banks of culm and Blue Mountain hills and sky, she said, When all creation has ceased to groan, Ondro, when all creation has ceased to groan, and he walked around the ruts of water iced over on the road, the mountain to the east a shale silhouette against the graying sky, and he could see their outlines standing and waiting by the headframe, the miners, their butties, and Ruka, the one-armed Ruthenian who worked the lift, all of them waiting for the inside boss to give the signal and the cage to rise, and he yawned in the cold and quickened his step and put the bare hand that did not carry his growler inside his overalls because he no longer carried the big sprag he used to carry when he went down as a spragger, and he looked up again at the men as he approached the line and in those few feet realized he could see them more clearly, though he knew each one of them from the mine, could see the hats they wore with their lamps yet unlit at their peaks, the canvas coats on their hunched shoulders that even in the lightlessness still shone an inky black, and their own tin growlers, some of which he knew had beer in them and nothing else and which they carried by handles creaking like signs hanging in the wind outside the company store, could see them as he approached in the first morning of the last year of the decade there would be mules and cars stopped by sprags and lamps lit with carbide wicks in that mine, and he shivered in the coat that did not fit him anymore, yawned again and looked ahead at the mountain face materializing in the dawn, the patch having gone to sleep under skies overcast and threatening but waking to a front that left only a wind blowing in sharp gusts, and he fingered the beads of the rosary in his pocket, the rosary his mother had given him for his birthday the year after his father died, and he thought maybe there was time to say an Ave Maria to himself as he approached, but he walked faster and hoped the signal would sound as soon as he took his place in line

II

AND I WAKE HERE TO THE SOUND OF TERRITORIAL robins from the open window before the sun even breaks the horizon to the east of the pond and the whisper of breeze out of the cool night into a warming day approaching autumn, no blasts or buzzers or humming breakers, though creation has not ceased to groan, and I rise from my bed and go into the kitchen and lift the stove lid with the lifter to raise a small fire for my tea and breakfast with the coals that have burned down overnight, even though it is late August, raise them back to life with some birch-bark kindling and wood I cut and split last fall and will have to do again this fall before winter, and the fire catches and the sound of wind is the sound of draft down the flue to the firebox, and I place a kettle for hot water on the stove and leave it and go wash my face and put on a clean shirt and trousers and slide my rosary into my pocket and come back to the kitchen, and by now the sun has risen in the east above the hills that a half hour ago were an old familiar shale silhouette, and its first rays are reflected on the rippling, though still glassy, surface of the pond, and I can see it will be a clear morning, but I don't know what the afternoon will bring, and a long time ago I carried a dark wholly absent of light, like a beast carrying its burden along a steel track, year after year, through the patch, where they despised me, through school, where they derided me, through work at the brewery, where I found a new burden, and into prison, where I found my freedom not just from the burden but from the war, until I came here to New Hampshire because of a man named Jacobson, and I slept the first night and woke before dawn and set to my work of looking in the distance from the mountain they call Monadnock for the smoke of fires, and the day arced through and after two seasons and the war I left that lookout but did not leave the place of the mountain, I moved to a house on a pond that lies in the shadow of the mountain and worked in the guard shack as a ranger and never thought they might come to me, the children who have grown and have children themselves, though some were still in their mothers' bellies when we went down into the mine that day, because their parents no doubt told them I was and was not to blame and so why go into a past where nothing and no one can be reclaimed, until the last day I worked in that guard shack, the day I thought I would walk home as an old man free to live out his days far from the place he prayed remained in the past unclaimed, when the first three found me with the tenacity of generations or ghosts to haunt, I could not decide, and I brought them here and we sat on the big porch in the shadow of the mountain and they didn't even know how to ask the questions they had come to ask, but I knew, and after a while I told them I could still see the boy of thirteen on that morning of the first day of the year 1929, and I could tell them, if they wanted me to, what his life was like growing up in the mining patch outside of Hazelton, Pennsylvania, with his mother in the small house they rented from the company, how he missed the father he barely knew, how he worked because he believed he had to, and how he, the boy, went down into that mine and never emerged, the boy, whom I can still see, even today, but I knew it was the others they wanted me to tell them about, the others I had to carry with me, the husbands and fathers and grandfathers, had to carry with me and think of and have sometimes spoken of in what I have done and in what I have failed to do for those who knew them, who loved them, who missed them too for their entire lives and wondered what they said in their last moments that stretched to minutes and hours and days after we stood by the headframe and the January skies lightened and the dawn dispersed and the miners John Chibala and Štefan Bozak and their butties Matty and Emil heard the sound of the buzzer startling and loud in the cold and low-cloud air, and I slowed my steps as I reached the line and the miner John Chibala turned and greeted me by my first name and told me the inside boss said I would be going down with them in the cage that day as mule boy, and I shouldn't worry because he knew I already knew the mines from my work as a nipper and a spragger, and leading a mule was a big step up, but if Mr. Bartle-Jones said I was ready, then I was ready

And if you need anything, Ondro, anything at all, just ask, because today Štefan and I are going down to rob them pillars on breast number seven and it won't take the whole day, if it does we're too slow or too scared and we're neither, so we'll eat lunch in the mine but we'll be up top before the shift buzzer, ňestaraj śe, he said

and he spoke like that in his Šariš Slovak, the words rushed and fluid like water from a tap, his confidence and smile as infectious as the grippe, and he put his hand on my shoulder when he told me not to worry, and I said I had heard that Wicked was a piece of work, but I had seen and been around a lot of mules and I knew Wicked could do what was needed to get done for the cars and the coal he and Štefan Bozak would need to get up top, and my mother had given me a carrot to coax the beast, and John Chibala nodded and touched the peak of his cap

You sound pretty sure of yourself, he said

and I put my head down and he took his hand

from my shoulder and gave me a sock in the arm and laughed, and even there in the gray dawn his teeth shone like white marble

Your mother's a good woman, he said

and we all stood in line and waited for the cage in silence, the mines no mystery to me before that day because, although she had kept me from the ranks of the breaker boys when my father died in '24, my mother could only make so much money sewing the clothes miners and their butties wore and wore, and I remember when one of the foremen came to her in the kitchen of our house in the patch and told her I'd be going down to work as a nipper, a boy who opened and closed the shaft doors when the coal cars and their spraggers jockeyed through like one-eyed engines in the dark, just like she asked, and her face showed neither relief nor surprise

Until he gets used to it, the dark, and then maybe I can see my way to finding him a job as a spragger, the man said

and I didn't like the way he said maybe, and I looked at my mother as he spoke to her and she moved slowly at the stove, and when I looked back he had a smile on his face I also didn't like, and he saw me watching him

What d'ya think about that, son, he said

All right, sir, if you believe I can, I said

and he told me it had nothing to do with belief

but with how a kid worked and I said all right again, but I didn't feel all right standing there in the kitchen of our house in the patch, my mother quiet and staring at the stove, and the next day I went down in a cage full of men and boys in the shift and tried to pretend I wasn't scared, but two boys I knew who were spraggers, tough boys who would bully anyone who wasn't a miner or a butty, nudged each other and one of them made his way next to me in the cage

Don't piss yourself down there, he said

and he laughed and his breath smelled of old onions and his body of stale sweat and when he smiled his teeth were pitted with black, and a fear I had never felt before began to rise in me, but it wasn't hard, the work of a nipper, listening for the rumble of a car and watching for the carbide light of the mule boy at its head and the spragger running alongside, that's when I had to push open the door and let the car through and pull it shut again and wait in the dark for the next one, the wind around the edges and at the top and bottom of the door the only thing different or even distinctive from the absence of light every nipper sat in all day, and I sat there all day minding the door that I had to open when the cars came and keep shut for ventilation when they did not, it was the dark that was hard, dark that in the complete absence of light was like a presence itself, dark you could feel because you had to feel where you were, because even if you put your hand right next to your face you couldn't see it, you could only feel it when you pressed your fingers against your eyes and cheeks so that you knew at least you had a hand that could touch your face, that kind of dark, and I sat there in it while I waited for the coal cars, and I sat there in it when there were no cars, and I sat there in it by myself and cried and cried because I couldn't move without wondering what was around me except the door, where I felt the wind at the top and bottom swirling like they told kids ghosts swirled, and I thought of the priest talking about the Holy Ghost as a wind and the wisdom that came on that wind, and I wondered how many people I knew who had died were ghosts, though I never wondered if my father was a ghost, he was full of muscle and strong, so strong he used to carry me off to bed by holding his arm out straight and saying, Pome het, in the Šariš every Slovak in the mines spoke, and I'd grab on and hold tight and he'd carry me dangling like that into my small bedroom in our small house in the patch, his arm one long rope of muscle, so I knew he wasn't a ghost, but the dark and the wind made me wonder and brought me close to fear, and I sat there for a long time in the wind, sat there even after I heard the shift buzzer sound and no more cars came down the track and I couldn't move to make my way through the dark and the wind, and I wondered if I could sit there until the next day, sleep when I wanted to sleep, wake when I had to wake, what did it matter whether it was day or night without any light, I told myself, until I saw the flicker of a carbide coming down the tracks and I could tell by its height it was Mr. Bartle-Jones, the inside boss, and the light got brighter and I could see where I was, see the light reflected in the black anthracite of the ceiling and the water along the floor of those tracks, and he hollered for me by name and told me it was time, I should get home and cleaned up and ready for tomorrow, and I wiped my eyes as I swung my arm around to pick up my growler bucket so that he wouldn't see that I'd been crying, and I followed him down the tracks to the cage, and I did that for a year, until that same foreman, the one who had given me the job before, came by again when my mother and I were sitting down to dinner one night, and he joined us and told my mother mid-meal that one of his spraggers had lost an arm horsing around, the same boy, I realized as the foreman spoke, who told me not to piss myself, and he said if her son wanted the job I could have it, and she knew a spragger made considerably more than a nipper because spraggers got tipped by the miners whose cars they followed and braked and made sure none of the coal fell out or was stolen before it went up top and was weighed and emptied fairly, and I looked over at my mother but she never looked up from her plate, and I looked back at the foreman, who turned to me with that same smile on his face as he chewed our food and belched from the beer he had been drinking before he came into our house

Well, what d'ya think of that, son, you wanna be a spragger and make a little extra money in them there mines, he said

and he sounded as though my mother wasn't listening or hadn't heard

Thank you, yes, sir, I'll take the job, I said

You're damn right you will, he said

and he finished eating and put his fork down and picked up his glass and gulped the water, then stood and threw his napkin on the table and walked out of the house, and my mother never looked up or away from her plate, and I went into the mine the next day with a sprag stick as a spragger, and I did the job the way I'd always seen it done, it wasn't hard, and after I had gotten accustomed to the dark I grew to love the mines, and even though I believed it was the kind of work my mother wanted for me, the better pay, the relief that we would not be beholden to the company, though everyone was beholden to the company in some way, I would have done it regardless, because a spragger was given a carbide lamp and I went from stationary and watchful in the dark at the doors to something resembling a cross between a trapeze artist and quarterback for the Pottsville Maroons with my sprag, a kind of club that was a little over a foot long and weighed about three pounds, and I used it to slow or stop the coal car by jamming it into the wheels of the load as it coursed along the gangways in the dark through doors where nippers sat and to the bottom of the slopes that took each load to the surface, where it was weighed and emptied, and if a spragger went too slow he slowed up the other cars, too fast and the cars collided with doors, or the spragger lost an arm when he tried too late to make that sprag do what he brought it down into the mine to do, or he killed the mule and the mule boy out ahead of the car, and no one wanted to kill a mule, they were more valuable than the boy, and I had a few close calls, broke a collarbone, broke a finger, and lost more than one toenail, but I did my job well and at the age of twelve I was at home in the mines, took home my pay and gave it to my mother and she got what food we needed at the store and never had to pay on credit, and she stopped sewing, at least the clothes of other miners and butties, and I believed it was all because I had become a man who knew the work of the mines, and yet I was still too young to understand why four months after I became a spragger my mother's belly had grown round and in another month she told me she was going to have a child, still too young to understand how so many years after my father had died this could be so, but her silence kept me and everyone else in the patch silent, even the priest, until weeks later, how many I don't know, I came home from the mine on a day sometime around when I turned thirteen and my mother was in bed and a doctor was there and an old widow we called Babča was cleaning blood from the floor, and the doctor told me my mother needed rest and walked out the door, and when I asked Babča what had happened to the baby, she shook her head

There isn't a baby anymore, take your mother some tea and sit with her, she said

and on the twenty-third of December that year Mr. Bartle-Jones, the inside boss, called me into his office before I went up top, and I didn't understand why, only miners spoke with the boss, and he took his hat off and stood by his small table in that room carved out of stone and framed in timber

I need you to lead Wicked when we go back to work first of the year, he said

and I shivered a little

Kicked that Stepinack boy's head clean in yesterday, maybe you heard, he said

and I had but I didn't say anything, I just waited because Wicked was named for the kind of mule he was, had done the same to another boy and once chased the butty of a miner clear down a gangway until he was nearly run over by a car, and I knew mule boy was a good job, but working with Wicked was about like knowing when there was going to be a cave-in, and as though he knew what I was thinking, Mr. Bartle-Jones told me the Stepinack boy was alive, and I wanted to say I can't

It's not the mule, son, it's the way you treat him, and I'd have a hundred Wickeds if I could, it comes with a good raise and your mother won't have to go back to sewing clothes, he said

That foreman told you to give me this job, I said

and I shouted it a little too loud in the office carved out of stone, and Mr. Bartle-Jones put his head down and raised it again and spoke in about as soft a tone as I've heard a man speak in the mines

No, son, that foreman got transferred by the company to another colliery in the west of the state, I'm giving you this job, he said

and he put his head down again and pinched the brim of his cap and we were both quiet, so that I could hear the sound of water dripping from the ceiling somewhere outside the office

It'll be all right, Ondro, I'll send you down with John Chibala, he said

and on the first day of 1929 I went down into the mine not with a sprag in hand but with a carrot in my growler for Wicked the mule, and in the pocket of my overalls that day, as they are in my pocket still, I kept the rosary my mother had given me on my eighth birthday, my father's rosary, and she told me that he had made the beads himself when he was a boy and his father told him they were moving to America and he should thank God for this gift, the opportunity to travel over the ocean to a place where they would no longer have to live in a hut but would live in a house, one his father said he would build himself with wood from the trees that grew along the sides of mountains in America, and he could keep bees and grow grapes and vegetables and they would have meat on their table because he would buy a rifle and hunt and dress the game and put it on that table for the entire family to eat, and all of this would be as he said because there was work in America for any man who wanted to work, and if you worked you were blessed by God, and the day before they climbed onto a wagon that took them to the train that took two days to get to the boat my father took a hatchet to the limb of an ash tree in the churchyard when the priest was on his rounds and fashioned the beads of the rosary from the limb of that tree as they sailed across the ocean to America, and as my mother told me this story about my father I unwrapped the brown paper in which she had wrapped the gift and touched the twisted horsehair string and oblong beads that had turned black from my father's fingers, turned black from the coal he handled and the sweat of that work, and I held the rosary up to the window light and listened to my mother laugh like she hadn't laughed for a year, and then, still smiling, she wondered out loud how my father kept himself from bringing the whole tree to America, he loved the old country so much, and she looked out of the window too at the slag heaps in the patch and the breaker in the distance and back at me

Sometimes I used to hold it just to hold him again, she said

and she leaned over me where I sat in the chair

You see where it's a little darker and smoothed down, from the sweat and oils of the man, she said

and I did see where it was darker and smoothed down, but I didn't understand then what she was trying to tell me about holding him, and she could tell I didn't understand, and her smile disappeared

Happy birthday, Ondro, she said

and she touched my head like the priest touched my head when he gave me a blessing at Communion, and she walked to the stove, where she kept a pot of hot water, and poured it over her infusion of dried strawberry leaf and chamomile, and I put the rosary in the front pocket of my trousers, and it has never left there, except when it came out during Lent or the months of May and October, when my mother and I said the rosary after dinner every night, and that's where it was when I waited in line that day, my first day going down as mule boy, and John Chibala greeted me and said ňestaraj śe, but I wasn't worried and I didn't pray, not even the Ave Maria I had thought of starting, I just ran my fingers over the smooth and blackened beads I had probably made a little smoother in those five years they had been mine, not because I wanted to hold the man who had made the rosary but because I didn't want to be distracted from the work I was going down to do for the first time, and as I was thinking about this work and worrying those beads, one of the butties in line, John Chibala's butty Matty, said that the girl the butty Emil had gone to a dance with the Saturday before looked to him like an angel out there on the dance floor, and a girl like that was going to leave the patch and do something one day, become a teacher or marry a guy from Williamsport who didn't know what the hell a mine looked like inside, and Emil stared at Matty as he spoke, and I could see something like pride and confusion in his eyes

She won't be leaving me, not now, Emil said

and Emil put his head down and toed the frozen ground, and Matty knew something I couldn't know, he put his arm around his friend's shoulder and told him to be careful, he was lucky to have found such an angel in the patch and these things worked out

Look at me, our kid's a year old already, Matty said

and Emil thanked him and the look of confusion at least sneaked away, and Štefan Bozak shushed them and told them there would be plenty of time to talk at the end of the shift, and I kept rolling those beads between my thumb and forefinger and would have begun to say a decade for Emil and his angelic girl, for Matty and his young child and wife, for Štefan Bozak and his brood of kids, and for John Chibala and his daughter Magda, but the lift engaged and the cable hummed and after a while the cage surfaced and John Chibala said, Pome het, and I let go of my rosary and took my hand out of my pocket, and it occurs to me now that I have never thought to say so much as a single Ave of the rosary since that day, I can read the prophet Jonah in Hebrew because Jacobson taught me in prison, and I have read his translations from the Greek of Parmenides, and my favorite course in the college of engineering was a course on Shakespeare, but I don't know that I could remember how to begin the Ave Maria, though I have had my rosary with me every day of my life, except when I was in prison and they kept it with the other personal effects, but this morning I sip my tea and reach into the pocket of my trousers and clench the first of the smaller, close-together beads, and imagine I am with my mother in the patch house, around the table after dinner in the month of May, Ave Maria gratia plena, I think, yes, and I am as grateful for the mornings at the end of summer here as I was for the coming of summer in those days, both seasons holding that gradual warming of the sun after a night of cold that is no longer or not yet freezing, Dominus tecum, because the cold of winter was more of a hardship then in the patch house when I woke to snow and freezing cold in my room and pulled the woolen blanket around me tighter before I jumped out of bed and dressed in my cotton dungarees and canvas coat and ran down to the kitchen as fast as I could to get to the stove and the breakfast of toast and tea my mother made for me, benedicta tu in mulieribus, I don't miss it, that cold in the patch house, because although winter here is so severe I often wonder if it will ever end, even when I can see the light changing and the deep snows melting and the birds beginning to sing again, my stove is better than the one on which my mother cooked, et benedictus fructus, and this house has been built with horsehair in the lathe of the walls and a cellar for a foundation, where I keep my vegetables and meat in barrels I've acquired, so that nothing will freeze in the winter or spoil in the summer as it did when we were able to get milk or eggs or a side of bacon from the company store, ventris tui, which is not unlike being down in the mines too, now that I think of it, the mines were also warm in the winter and cool in the summer, the temperature of an autumn day in October, or an Easter Sunday in April, or the cellar of a house in New Hampshire all year round, and that was true every day regardless of the season, and once I learned what I would find down there in the dark, the temperateness of the mines became a place of peace I found in that place of work, and I understood in some way why men went down there for their pay, some to make a difference in their lives, some just to survive, Sancta Maria, mater Dei, but in everyone there was skill in the labor and purpose in the outcome because they said if the miner stops mining, the entire world would come to a halt, and the companies knew a miner was not simply pulled off the street and sent down to work, a miner was made, crafted, the kind of skilled worker who carries the progress of the world on his back and greases the machine of that progress with his blood, ora pro nobis peccatoribus, so they said, and listen to me, still sounding like the bosses who used to spew those lines out like smoke, but they weren't wrong, I knew that the ones who knew this place of temperateness would sooner be buried in those mines than burned on a shop floor or maimed in a slaughterhouse or watch their children die of hunger while they picked fruit in the sun for someone else, nunc et in hora mortis nostrae, yes, that's it mostly, and I can feel the rosary in my pocket still as I pray for no reason other than that the words are a memory to me and I can touch the oblong beads that long ago absorbed my father's touch, and my mother's touch when she held them, wanting to touch him, as she told me she did when once she wondered out loud if I had lost my faith

Faith in what, I said

and she was quiet for a moment

In what I know you carry with you every day, like you're waiting for someone, she said

and she was right, though it's not like when we waited in line for the cage to rise, or when we waited in the dark for the searchers to find us, no, it's the waiting of another kind, like someone waiting for a train, a bus, a letter, or sometimes for a season, to arrive, the counting down of ordinary time, and though some have said there can be no faith in anything that is not God, God too knew waiting, knew it like a desire and a need, knew it when he summoned a prophet, the Navi, as Jacobson said when we studied Jonah, and one suffered and many were changed by it, and I am an old man now, changed by everything and nothing, waiting only to return to the ground, as the others have, and I think of Jacobson when I am sitting here and not praying but touching the rosary my parents touched, and waiting, I think of the Hebrew he taught me and I can still read, the prophet Jonah his favorite book and the lines he copied out in Hebrew and gave to me when we parted, because he said I was Navi, whether I wanted to be or not, and I assured him I did not, but that only made him smile and insist it was not if but when, and that was a long time ago, and I am hungry now after my tea and I think I will fry an egg, so I lift the stove lid with my lifter and feed more wood into the firebox, and the wind that fans the fire toward the wood in that firebox of the stove is a fierce sort of sliver of breath from the breeze outside and reminds me each time of the wind that came with the lift of the cage to the surface, always a wind, as though it had pushed that cage from below straight to the top in concert with the cable that hauled and lowered it day after day, and it happens again and again, I will hear something or see something and my mind will go back, and it is that wind down the flue and into the firebox today that conjures Ruka, the one-armed Ruthenian, throwing back the gate and John Chibala and his butty Matty and Štefan Bozak and his butty Emil all walking in, and I am last, and Ruka touches each of us on the shoulder as though counting

Don't get used to it down there, he says

Or what, old man, John Chibala says

Or I'll have to come down and see what's keeping you, Ruka says

and he leans for the latch and closes the gate and I can see his face because morning has come and with it more light, see what I always saw when we went down, an old man who worried when we left and rejoiced when we came back, and the buzzer sounds and the cage jolts and begins to drop, and a wind that is warm in winter and cool in summer pushes up from the depths, not as though it is rushing to get out but because it is the wind of the mines and will return to the mines, and it pushes against the bottom of the cage for a moment, then circles around as the cable catches to control our descent and the wind begins to whisper in from the top as the cage drops and the whispers become like howls from the sides and the top, the entire descent a chorus of howling wind and cable and cage as we drop, all of us silent there amid the howling, lights of the shaft blinking as we pass, lights of the new electrical lines and lights from men's hats as they shine for a moment from the dark of the gangways we pass, the speed steady, the distance lengthening, until it all becomes too constant, too ordinary, too far, and the cage keeps dropping and dropping, and I used to wonder each time without fail just how far down into the earth a cage and its cable could drop, how far down into the earth the work of mining could go, until I was certain that every man who ever made the descent with cables and coal cars and mules wondered in his heart, regardless of where he stood with God when he saw the priest in the confessional, if this was Hell into which he was descending, the wind, the whispering, the darkness, the blinking fires, the endless, endless, endless falling, just as I heard the priest once describe it in his sermon on Good Friday, and then the cage began to slow and come to a stop, and a wind that's never seen the sky rushed in through the door as the miner John Chibala opened it and walked out, then Štefan Bozak, the butties Matty and Emil, and me, the mule boy, and the wind gave us one last push there in the chamber, as if to send us down the gangways and shafts and into the breasts of the mine, and John Chibala closed the door behind us, the buzzer sounded, and the cage rose again, rose to the surface as though it understood its own call to work, rose to where it would pull more miners and their butties back down, over and over, hour after hour, day after day, until creation has ceased to groan, and when I sat down to tell those who came in search of me so many late summers before about their own fathers, what they said that day, what they did and what they failed to do, I always began by telling them first that my father died in the same mine, butty to a miner on his last day as butty having earned the right to be called a miner himself, young though he was, because the man he worked for that day was robbing pillars he had not been told to rob, my father the last one in the exhausted seam when the roof came down, and they were able to pry him out and bring him up and lay him on a board for the doctor to see, then went to summon my mother from the house in the patch and told her she needed to get up to the colliery, and she knew what had happened, she told me later when I had asked her what my father's last words were, if he even had any, and she dropped everything and put me in a chair at the kitchen table and told me not to move, she'd be back soon, and she ran up to the colliery and into a back room where my father was laid out, his arm twisted, his head and face flattened and bloodied and turned to the side so that she thought he was dead already, but the doctor said in the voice of a man who seemed tired of gazing on scenes like these that he'd make a full recovery, in time, and my father turned his one good eye to my mother and tried to speak, and so she lowered her head to his and he whispered, Anna, tonight I will be with God, protect our child, and he said protect our child, my mother told me then, not because he thought I was a child but because she was in the middle days of her pregnancy, and she took his hand and kissed it and told him to be strong, then ran down to the house in the patch to feed me and wash me and get me ready for bed, and when she went back up to the colliery she expected to see an ambulance or a delivery truck or anything there to take him to the hospital, but there was no ambulance, no truck, no one to tell her anything, except the foreman, who told her that her husband was dead, and the next day the other miners and their butties took the man's body down to the house in the patch, and I remember the cold in the house from the open door that had to come off the hinges to get the casket in, the sound of water and its constant splashing in the tub as they washed him, then the quiet and the weeping amid the prayers of the old Ruthenian priest as he chanted the Panakhyda for the dead, because my young father had been baptized in the old country in the Byzantine rite, and the brother I would have had was born still one month later and buried next to my father's grave in the cemetery of the Byzantine church, and my mother and I had nowhere else to go, so we stayed in the patch and she sewed the miners' clothes, until that foreman came to our house to give me a job as a nipper and I went down into the mine for the first time, though I never mentioned this to any of those who came to me and asked me about their fathers, not what the foreman did, nor did my mother and I ever speak about why she felt she needed to give in to the demands of the man who ran the mine, except for the night she rode the train to Wilkes-Barre after I had written her the week prior to say that I'd been drafted into the army now that our country was at war, and we had dinner at a small restaurant near Public Square and she asked what I was going to do and I told her I would go to prison rather than fight, even if she thought I was a coward, and she said it didn't matter what she or anyone else thought, and cowards aren't necessarily the ones who don't put up a fight

I lived in a prison after your father died, Ondro, she said

and she sipped her small glass of wine from the

bottle I had ordered for us both and placed it back on the table and never raised her eyes to look at me

No amount of fighting would have gotten me out, she said

and that was all she said, and I paid the bill and she stayed at a cheap hotel that night and left for Shenandoah again in the morning, and I have wondered about those words for the many years since she has gone to be with God herself, because she was right, no amount of fighting would have gotten me out of my sentence, I went to prison not for what I had done but for what I had failed to do, hidden in a room deep below the ground where I did not find God and God did not find me, and I have wondered if this is what I have been asked to carry for the rest of my life, if there is life in this, what little I have left from this summer day forward, if, as Jacobson said, I am Navi, and I don't know, except to say that it is aloneness, nothing more, I wish I had been rescued from, redeemed perhaps, as John Chibala's daughter Magda once called it, from my deep fear of the dark, not the dark in which there is no light but the dark in which there is nothing, no thing, not even the hand that rises to touch the face, and when I told Jacobson this in prison, he wondered out loud if there could be such a thing, no thing, as if any thing that is could somehow cease to be, and he quoted Parmenides from the text he had translated from Greek, Nothing is not, that is what I bid you consider, and I have thought a great deal about that and other things Jacobson said to me since the day I walked out of that prison, and I have come to believe there is no not being, and I will be of the earth one day as I am now, as my mother is and my father is and John Chibala and Štefan Bozak and their butties Matty and Emil, and Mr. Bartle-Jones, and even that foreman who was sent away and never seen again, even in the dark and even in the days of summer in this old mountain world to which I came to work to get out of prison and where I stayed when the war was over and they released me and I found this small house on a pond that sits to the east of the mountain, in those days I read from the prophet Jonah on Fridays and prayed in the evening every evening when there was no light and no one, save the lamp and the ghosts, because I still remembered how to pray, and I felt not the peace but the need to pray for a family I never had, creating an order I longed for and never found, and I waited for them in that dark to come to me, the revenants, just as I waited for their children to come to me in the long light of summer, and always for one thing, their desire, their need to know what happened, what was said, what I had done and what I had failed to do, and to each one of them I told the exact same thing at the start, we exited the cage and lit the lamps that sat at the peaks of our caps, and John Chibala walked with me to the stables, where we found Wicked in his stall, and he told me to go easy, but I knew, and the other mule drivers moved away from us as I reached into my growler and took out the carrot my mother had gotten at the company store and placed in there, and I held it up to Wicked's nose and he, I could tell Wicked was a he by the enormous penis that emerged beneath him when the beast got a whiff of that carrot, he stuck his tongue out to lick it and inhaled it in one motion of tongue and breath and chewed it up and sniffed my hand for another one, but I said in the Šariš my mother always spoke when I had had enough of what she was giving me, Al'e už dosc, and his head bobbed and I could see the ears worn down at the top from the anthracite and stone ceilings they had scraped across, and I opened the gate and led him out by the bridle and said, Už, and his head bobbed again, not a nod or nicker just a bob, and John Chibala was smiling under the light of his lamp

That's good, Ondro, these mules like to be spoken to in Slovak, my mother always used to say that God may speak Latin but the angels speak Slovak, he said

and he told me he had to get to work and that I was to bring old Wicked down shaft two, because they'd be setting up outside of breast number seven and Štefan was already in there with the drill and the butties with their picks and shovels and he had to get over there to time everything as they robbed those pillars, because it had to be done right or the whole ceiling would come down, and he had seen that happen to miners who didn't know or didn't care and that's what got them killed, and I told him I'd get Wicked hooked up to a train of cars and we'd be over there ready to take his coal up top, and he disappeared down the gangway, his light floating ahead of him, up and down with every step he took like a vertical pendulum in the dark, and I led Wicked out of the mule stalls and over to where a team of cars were, and the boss pointed to three and said those were reserved for Chibala and the work he was finishing in number seven, and he watched me as I led Wicked to the front of the cars and hooked up the harness and the bridle, and the boss asked me if I had a switch to hit the mule with and get him going, and I just shook my head

He'll go, I said

and I whispered, Pome het, and we headed down the gangway and into the shaft and I could hear them already at work when Wicked and I rumbled up to breast number seven, and it was a thing of beauty to watch John Chibala work in the mines, the sounds and shadows of the men inside that room like a play, or the ballet I once went to with Magda Chibala when we were both in college and the ballet had traveled from New York to Wilkes-Barre and we bought tickets, it was like that watching John Chibala work, every movement rehearsed and exact, no motion wasted, no movement made for anything except the extraction of coal that gleamed in the sharp lights of the carbide lamps like diamonds the earth had decided long ago they would never be, but somehow more beautiful not just in their allure but in their need, these chunks and blocks that the miners removed from ceiling to floor with the blow of a sledge then stood by listening to the ceiling as it settled, talking they called it, John Chibala and Štefan Bozak listening for any signs of weakness and collapse, and all the while their butties Matty and Emil shoveling and hauling the coal from those pillars, coal so pure and black it was clear why they robbed it rather than leave it there, out of the breast and into the cars that waited along the tracks in the gangway, and I had watched John Chibala when I was a spragger and thought the same then, wondering at the skill and the beauty of the work the man set his hands to, a good miner skilled enough to know what to do underground to the coal that would fill the car and head to the surface to bring in the money the boss was paying, a job as good and fair as anyone who worked for a daily wage with his hands could expect, and sometimes more, because a miner was his own business, his own man, the foreman coming by once a week because the mines were a big place and he couldn't be everywhere at once, so the miner was his own boss within a company of owners and foremen and bosses, and he bought his own clothes and tools and dynamite and blasting caps and paid his butty and tipped the spraggers and mule boys out of his own wage so that everyone made sure the car was topped and stayed topped as it headed to the surface and the breaker and the train cars that hauled it out of the colliery and down the line, and when the miner had brought to the surface all the coal he was expected to mine in a day, he went home, back to the patch to see his wife and his family and to take a bath and to eat his supper, and though the mines were dirty they were no dirtier than a shop floor or a tannery or a railyard, and no miner stayed dirty longer than was necessary, a miner worked but he knew his business and his business was what lay beneath the earth and the earth took good care of him, if he worked, and John Chibala and Štefan Bozak filled that train of three cars in what might have been two hours or so, and Wicked and I pulled them away and onto the gangway and down the tracks with a spragger running beside us through wind and doors where nippers sat in darkness all day, and the spragger stopped when we got to the slope, and we took them up and out of the mine and a worker chalked the cars as if to say I know whose cars these are, and Wicked and I turned around and took another shaft back to where there was another train of cars, and then back into the mine and down to the chamber where John Chibala and Štefan Bozak had just hammered a single mine timber up against a place in the roof of the breast they were robbing where both miners had thought it weakest

Let's take a break, John Chibala said

and all four sat down near the next pillar they would hammer out and opened their growlers and ate their bread and cheese, Štefan Bozak the one who had brought beer down in his growler, beer he made in his own house in the patch, just enough not to stir the interest of the authorities, it was said, but enough to make sure the inside boss and the inspector had two or three bottles on the weekend, and he passed it around to each of them for a sip, and Matty and Emil laughed and wiped their mouths with their sleeves and jostled each other as they ate, and I heard Matty ask Emil where at the dance he could have gone with his girl to get to know her better, and Emil didn't say anything, but if a man covered in coal dust could have blushed beneath the light of a carbide lamp, Emil blushed

You don't need to see a priest do you, Emil, Štefan Bozak asked

and he spoke from out of the harsh light of the four carbides that shined from the hats of all of them there at the entrance of the breast

That depends, Štefan, Matty said

Everyone sees the priest eventually, now let's go boys, it's moving fast, we'll be headed up top by lunchtime, John Chibala said and they all nodded and stood

Ondro, John Chibala said

and when I looked in his direction he reached into his growler and pulled a carrot out and pitched it across the sharp light to where I still sat on the edge of a car out on the gangway with the mule

Give that to Wicked and you'll never have a problem with him for as long as that beast lives, he said

and I thanked him and held it under the mule's nose and the mule sniffed and inhaled and ate the carrot all in the same breath, his enormous penis emerging like a turtle looking out of its shell, and Matty and Emil laughed and laughed at the mule's phallus, and Wicked just bobbed his head again and I patted him and let him smell my hand, and John Chibala was right, I never had another problem with Wicked the mule for as long as he lived, and I whispered, Pome het, and remembered the blacksmith stepping away from his forge that morning when he heard me greet Wicked in Slovak to tell me that the only man that mule had ever worked for without a hitch was old Stanley, who used to sing to him in Slovak, and when Stanley died in his sleep Wicked seemed to get angrier and angrier about anyone who tried to lead him, the Stepinack boy the last straw, and I couldn't sing worth a damn, I told him, but I knew Slovak, and I whispered to Wicked in Šariš all morning like my mother spoke to me at home and he did everything I asked him to do, and we loaded car after car out of that breast, hauling the coal John Chibala knew not to leave underground, because they knew what they were doing, John Chibala and Štefan Bozak, their butties Matty and Emil, and they reckoned they could be done by two o'clock that afternoon and call it a day and go up top, and Wicked and I were right there hauling the cars up the slope, then back to the opening of the breast, where the miners worked robbing those tall and wide columns of black, wider than any pine I've seen that survived the clear-cut, and there was nothing above this breast, so as they got close to lunch they started taking entire columns, beginning at the back and letting the rooms collapse as they retreated to the face, and they kept loading coal into the cars that Wicked and I brought back empty and ready to haul, the slow self-destruction of the room a wonder to behold as they let the breast down easy, Štefan Bozak would say, and the slabs in the darkened back of the room would not fall so much as fold from ceiling to ground like a barely lit horizon meeting the silhouette of a mountainside as the sun went down, the sound of it like thunder rolling, and they did this for hours that day, the haul steady and big, and they all knew they would be done before the shift boss called it, and Wicked and I were like an old team of mule and driver already, and we drove John Chibala's cars fast, sometimes faster than the spragger so we could return sooner for more and to be there when they took the last of their haul and that breast folded into its own final dark, and then they sat after a few more hours and took their lunch near a long open stretch of the gangway away from the breast this time, the ceiling all around in there talking to the mine, but the miners without fear of it, because the mule and the rats showed no fear of it, and John Chibala asked me to sit with them and eat what lunch I had for myself and my mule and I felt part of them, not one of them, part of them, then he stood

All right boys, let's get the last of it, he said

and I knew by boys he meant his butty Matty and Štefan Bozak and Štefan's butty Emil, not me, the mule boy, but I rose with them there on that long open stretch of gangway and patted Wicked's head and whispered, Pome het, and gave him a tug, his warm muzzle pushing softly against my back

III

AND ALTHOUGH I HAD TOLD ALL OF THIS TO Jacobson in prison, the first of the children came to the mountain to find me many years later, on my last day with the Forestry and Recreation Commission, my last day in the guard shack at the entrance to the trail up the saddleback of the mountain, an afternoon in late August when I knew there would be one of those summer storms so big the clouds rise up in the western sky like an erupting volcano, the air becomes thick with ozone, and the forest ticks with the sound of wildlife skittering for shelter, and they drove up in an old and hard-worn Plymouth station wagon about to boil over, drove up with the windows down, it was so hot, an older man, a younger man at the wheel, and a boy in the backseat looking like his father in that way the firstborn always does, and I recognized all three of them, recognized them right away, and before the younger man could even say anything I told him his radiator needed water and he stared down the hood of the car from inside and nodded, and I took a pail I kept by the steps of the booth and walked with it down to the creek that ran from the top of the mountain and into one of the ponds that lay to the east of the mountain, and I hoped he knew what I was doing, because it took me some time to walk down to the creek with the pail, cicadas whirring in one last chorus of heat before the rains began, and I wondered where I would start when he asked the question I knew he was going to ask, and I filled the pail at the creek side and walked a little slower back up the road with the cold water splashing over the sides and onto my hands and boots, and I don't know if they wondered where I was or where I had gone, but all three of them were still there in that Plymouth when I returned and they seemed neither bothered nor worried by how long it took me to walk down to the creek with a pail and return with it full of water, maybe the older man was trying to figure out how or where he would begin to ask what I knew he was going to ask, and I told the younger man at the wheel to pop the hood and he got out and undid the latch and lifted the hood and it was hot under there, so hot I had to unscrew the radiator cap with my hand holding on to my loose shirttail, and I could see the water was down more than half and the radiator was going to boil over if he drove that car more than a few more miles, and I poured the creek water sputtering and boiling right to the top of the radiator, and when it cooled I put the cap back on and closed the hood and told him that ought to do it for a while, and he said he was much obliged and was quiet for a minute, so I just waited

I'm looking for Ondro Prach, he said

and I nodded and told him he didn't have to look any further and I stood there and listened to him explain not why but from where they had come, the state of Pennsylvania, the town of Hazelton, the mining patch not far from where his grandmother had lived during the early years of her life, a place he had never known and hadn't even visited because it was nothing more than a ruin in the midst of slag heaps and culm banks and a big hulking breaker that rose up in the near distance like the husk of some long-dead monster, and when he was done, or sounded like he was done, I went over to the guard booth and closed the door and locked it and told him I was about to knock off for the day and in fact this was my last day at work and he and his son and his grandson ought to come on over to my place, we could talk there, and I began to walk down the hill along the dirt road

You know who I am, he said

and I stopped there in the road with my back to them, not because I realized it must have seemed strange that I was walking away after I had just invited them to my house but because it never occurred to me to get in a car and drive the mile distance home, and I turned around and walked back to their car

I know who you are, could tell the minute you drove up, could tell it by looking at all three of you, I said

and he said he was going to ask me how I knew the boy was his son but didn't have to now, and I said again that we could talk at my place, or rather, his father could ask his questions and I would try to answer them, or tell him what I think he wanted to hear, or maybe what he didn't want to hear

I can drive us over if it's far, he said,

and I told him it wasn't far, but maybe we should drive after all, otherwise he and his son and his father would have to walk back here to the guard booth to get his car, but I was just so used to closing up and walking home to my house, down the mountain and across the road to the pond, that I guess that's why I started out on foot, and he looked over at his son in the backseat and motioned with his head and his son moved over and opened the door and I got in and pulled the door shut and the man got in behind the wheel and turned the engine over and checked the heat gauge, and I looked over at the boy and asked him what his name was

Emil, he said

and I told him that was a fine name and he smiled, and I turned back to face the road and told the man to pull out, then take the first left he came to and drive about a mile, and he eased the clutch and pulled that Plymouth out onto the road and used his indicator there in the woods to make the left turn when we got to my road, and we drove along past the wetlands that had dried up some in the summer heat and the fields of long grass almost ready for mowing, both wetlands and grass no doubt looking forward to the rain coming, and I pointed to a space between a beech tree and a giant hemlock and told him to turn in there and we drove up the one-lane path to the house where I lived on the pond, and they stayed in the car when I got out and walked to the door, so I turned to see why they weren't following me and walked back over and leaned into the rolled-down window of the passenger side, where the older man was sitting

I've got iced tea and lemonade in the house and it's nicer than sitting here, I said

and they seemed to be talking to each other, father and son

That sounds like just the thing on a day like today, the younger man said

and all three of them got out and walked with me up to the front door and we went into the house that isn't very big, just a living room and a kitchen with a table and a couple of bedrooms down the hall, and they stood there, already looking like they wished they were back on the road headed home, and I got lemonade for the boy, whose name was Emil, and was about to pour a glass for his father

You got something stronger than that for me, beer maybe, it sure has been a long drive, he said

and I told him I didn't, that I hadn't had a drop to drink since I got arrested for not going to the war and becoming a conscientious objector, and besides, I had had my fill of beer working at the brewery in Wilkes-Barre, and plenty of whiskey when I wasn't working there and was trying to run away from the people and things I wanted to run away from, so no, I told him I was sorry but I didn't have any beer, but I could walk over to the hotel if he wanted some that badly and find some beer there, or whiskey even, if it was strong he wanted, but it would take some time and I'd come back wet as a muskrat with this storm coming, or he could drive, I told him almost as an afterthought, because I had already forgotten that we had driven in his car, and he laughed and said iced tea was fine if that was what I was pouring, and so I poured him one, and I poured his father one, who hadn't said anything this whole time, and I poured another one for myself, and we took our drinks and I led them through a side door out onto a porch I had built that faced the mountain under an old and towering white pine that had somehow escaped the clear-cutting from over a hundred years ago, and I stood facing the mountain as the storm clouds grew, and they didn't know what it was I was going to do, what it was I would tell them about the butty Emil, one's father, the other's grandfather, the boy's great-grandfather, until lightning flashed from out of those clouds, then a clap of thunder so loud the boy whimpered almost and moved close to his father's side and the man hugged his son as though he feared the thunder more, and the rain came down like Heaven itself had breached the sky and we stood watching from under the porch roof and the white pine

That's what it sounded like underground that day, the collapse of the room from the breach to the gangway, I said

You still remember, the older man said

and I could hear the quaver in his voice even as we both had to speak louder to be heard above the roar of that rainfall on the roof and ground, and I just nodded, and we all sat down on chairs I had made from the stump ends of trees I bucked the year before and watched the rain, torrents of rain, the sound of it like coal running through a breaker chute, the noise something we could not speak above, only listen to, until it began to slow, as these storms do, almost as quickly as they begin, and when I didn't have to speak above a yell I took a deep breath and a sip of my tea and told them about the morning in '29 and why I was in the mine with the miners John Chibala and Štefan Bozak and their butties Matty and Emil, and when I said the name Emil the boy looked up as though he had realized why it was they had come here, and I told them that when all four of those men finished their lunches that day and rose and walked inside the breast where they were robbing the pillars, the miner John Chibala reckoned there was exactly one more load to go, because he knew how much coal he was going to get with the last of those pillars he robbed, and he knew that it would fill right to the bumpers the three cars I had hitched up to Wicked the mule, and they all went in there with their drills and sledgehammers and shovels, the roof talking so that even I could hear it, but John Chibala said the roof always talked when you got down to the last pillars of coal and so none of them was worried by it, and I stood at the entrance of the breast on the gangway and could see Štefan Bozak stop and survey the roof, and he called over to John Chibala and pointed out that if they carved not the nearest but the pillar that was one support in, the largest pillar, carved it slow and last, they could rob the others without the entire thing coming down, because the slab at the entrance was all one piece and the supports from the gangway would hold the opening up, and John Chibala nodded and they told Matty and Emil what they were going to do, and so the butties moved back from the inside and John Chibala and Štefan Bozak took their drills and sledgehammers in to where the next-to-the last support held up what there was to hold up in that room, and they began to carve away at it from the top and work their way down, and Wicked and I stood by at the face and watched the butties Matty and Emil bringing out the loads in shovels, some big slabs by hand, filling up the cars with them, the sound of anthracite on iron almost deafening in that close space underground, watched them and waited for them to load the last of the coal into the cars Wicked and I had brought back, and when I think of it now it makes sense to me, though it made no sense to me then, they hauled that pillar larger than a pine away in blocks and the ceiling folded slowly from the back to the entrance of the breast, and John Chibala and Štefan Bozak went at it with drills and sledges to be done with it, and I could see then by the light of the carbide that Štefan had all of a sudden noticed the ICC-14 box of American Cyanamid dynamite his butty Emil had left farther back in the room when they came out of the breast to take their lunch, and he seemed to want to call out, then thought better of it, counting no doubt the cost of the contents of the box and the pace with which the ceiling folded toward the ground, neither one worth the time to slide in there and pull that box out, but Emil saw it too and did his own reckoning, the speed with which he could move and the cost that would come out of his pay, because whatever was in that ICC-14 box of dynamite would come out of the miner Štefan Bozak's pay, and Emil bent low and moved fast toward the back of the room just as Štefan shouted, Zochap tak! because there wasn't time then to say much of anything, and Emil turned and in the corner of my eye I could see Wicked stamp a bit and twitch his ears like he wanted to move, like he wanted to go forward, but forward for him meant straight into what was left of that breast, and then in the sharp light of the miners' and their butties' carbides I could see the roof begin to come down, a slow fold at first, or so I thought, but it could not have been slow, no, it was fast, too fast, and that was when John Chibala had just taken a sledgehammer to the last of those pillars, taken it to a section at the bottom where he had taken out his drill, like when you cut a tree down and notch the trunk with the saw in a deep vee on the side where you want it to fall, then take the saw to the opposite side and cut, and you can drop that tree on a pine needle touching a bark beetle's ass, and that's what John Chibala had done to the last pillar, but a mine isn't a forest and a pillar isn't a pine, and every man and boy in there affects the air and weight and feel of the place, and I stopped speaking then and turned to the older man sitting on the stump end next to me with his grandson huddled at his side, the rain coming down off the roof in a trickle

You need to know one thing about your father, I said

and I waited for a long time before I went on, waited as I conjured that day again in my mind, the cold morning up top, the stamping feet in the line, the elevator descent, the men who seemed like men to me but who were no more than boys, younger than I was when I met the son, grandson, and great-grandson of the butty Emil, far younger than I am now

Your father told Matty, and in that way all of us, how much he loved your mother and thanked God for her because she was so beautiful, an angel Matty called her, and your father said yes, an angel, and yet she had chosen him over anyone she could have chosen and so he would get the chance to live his whole life with an angel sent by God, I said

and the son of the butty Emil listened to the last of the rain until it was only drops of water dripping from the roof to the ground by the time he spoke again, and he said his mother always held the memory of his father in a place of sadness and longing, and that was probably why she never married, and they left the patch when he was old enough to go to school because she had gotten a job as a teacher at a Catholic school in McAdoo, and she held that job right up until he graduated from high school and went to work with the post office in Hazelton and got married and, after a long time of trying, he and his wife had a son, and they raised him and one day he went off to college and got married and had this guy and they were grandparents, and he looked down at his grandson, who looked tired sitting there on the stump next to his grandfather in the afternoon light, the storm having tapered off completely, so that I could see the clouds swirling in the west above the mountain the way they swirl in the summer before a new high-pressure front comes in after the low to blow them out before sunset

She had died long before that, but I used to ask her about him all the time when I was growing up, and she would only tell me to forget the mines, nothing good ever came out of them, not even my father, he said

I heard she never married, I said

You would have known if you grew up in the patch, he said

I left when I could, when you were five maybe, but I had seen her with you, I said

I remember your mother but not you, your mother was good to her, the only one, the only one who didn't remind her with silence that she had sinned with him, he said

and I looked over at his son, the younger man, who looked so much like his father, a man who had gone to college and had probably never known what hard work felt like

They only knew because he died and left her and you, I said

and he nodded as if to say yes

But I've often wondered, growing up there, when I was old enough to know better, wondered not how but where they could have met and courted and, well, sinned, he said

In the patch, I said

Not from what I've seen of the place, he said

and his voice had the incredulity of those who cannot believe their parents were ever young

At the dance, the church in Hazelton, the feast of Christ the King on the Saturday night before, I said

Where they met, he said

No, they had met in the summer, I remember seeing Emil talking with her at the August picnic, but the dance is where she and Emil couldn't just hold hands any longer, I said

and he sat in his chair and sipped his tea and I could tell he was counting

You were born in late August, happy birthday by the way, and it was no sin, I said

and he nodded and we listened to the birds begin to sing again, the sun still having a long way to go before it dipped behind the mountain

The priest used to walk around and say to the boys and girls who were Emil and your mother's age, Leave room for the Holy Ghost, I said

and I told them that my mother was asked to chaperone those dances and she would take me and I would sit in a chair off to the side, and I wondered why there would be ghosts at a dance, but now I know, and I remember not seeing Emil for a long time that night, and then he was dancing again with her for the last song, the two of them smiling and close, because my mother said to him, Emil, remember the Holy Ghost, and Emil and his girl held each other at arm's length then, until the song was over and my mother told me it was time to go home

She would never tell me even that much, he said

Of course not, I said

and he touched the arm of his grandson Emil and looked out at the sun bending west toward the top of the mountain, rays slanting long and bright as they touched the edge of clouds broken up and moving away, and his face was a face of emptiness, no recognition, no revelation, no memory coming into focus, no, his face reflected the long afternoon light and nothing else

Well, that's more than I came here for already, he said

and he spoke this to his son, it seemed to me, because the younger man looked up at him as if to ask if it was time for them to go, but I knew what it was he had come here for, and I told him he needed to know that his father could not say much in the end when it came

Tell me what they were, those last words, he said

and I turned a little uncomfortably on my pine-stump chair

It's not easy for me, because it's been so long, and because I'm afraid I'm going to get less right than I will get wrong, I said

But you were there, he said.

and it wasn't a question, as though he doubted me, it was more of an admonition, as though I had a duty to sit and tell him how his father spent his last minutes, how he looked, how he said what he might have said, how it was he, the man before me, had grown up and become a man without him

Yes, I said

and I told him that John Chibala and Štefan Bozak were right and wrong about the capacity for the pillar closest to the entrance of the breast to hold up the ceiling as they retreated, because as the back of the breast collapsed in that place where the ICC-14 box of American Cyanamid dynamite lay, and where the butty Emil had gone to retrieve it, that movement created in the way the earth shifts and almost echoes everywhere in the mines enough movement to trigger the ceiling in its growing weakness to fail, except for the section where Štefan Bozak had thought to prop up and hammer in a support beam mid-breast, the roof coming down everywhere around us except in that ten-by-ten space, and I would have been killed outright had I not been standing where I was just ahead of Wicked at the entrance of the breast, but as I watched and felt the roof coming down on top of us, something made me, something compelled me, not to back away toward the gangway where Wicked still stood with his tipless ears twitching against the ceiling but to step into the room, and I stumbled toward the miners and their butties and got as far as John Chibala and Štefan Bozak, who stood beneath the pine beam as though they couldn't move, or wouldn't move, and I turned back to see Wicked in the new electric lights that ran along the gangway just before they went out, the entire slab and all of the ceiling and rock above it falling and Wicked stepping toward me, as if to follow me into the room, his large head and eyes seemingly blithe to the destruction around him one moment, the entirety of the beast buried beneath a deafening collapse of coal and rock the next, and the back of the breast, where Emil had gone to retrieve the box, collapsed in the same instant, the sound of rock on rock in that space of room, front and back, not like an explosion of damp, which comes presaged by a kind of whisper as it sucks the air out of a chamber into which it has crept, or from dynamite, which pushes the air back and through a chamber like a blow from a hammer, but as if it had formed the air into rock itself, wanting to fill the void the miners and their butties had created, fill it again in that instant as if to make the earth whole again, as if to punish the miners and their butties for believing they could take from those depths what belonged down there and bring it to the surface as their own, and everywhere around us was nothing but the roar of those rocks crashing down and the hollers of those men beneath it, as light became dark and that moment became our lives, and then silence, nothing but silence, and not just the silence from the fact that none of us could hear from the close proximity of the collapse but because everything stopped there in the mine, everything, even the groaning of the working ceiling, and through the dust and blackness I waited to see where I was, feel where I was, what I was, alive, yes, but where and on which side of whatever wall that collapse was surely to have built, and what that would mean for the hours or days I had left of my life, underground with those four men, if they had survived as well, and in the chokehold of the settling dust I could feel John Chibala lighting his lamp, so I knew that he was at least alive with me, and then I could see through that lighted dust where it was we stood, or I stood, cowering but standing, the others down, on knees, on backs, and by the light of John Chibala's lamp I surveyed the cell in which we huddled, the wall of rock where the entrance had been, the back of the breast where it was still dark, though the outline of rock from the ceiling floated through the dust, and there were groans not from that ceiling but from Emil, and then Štefan Bozak, who whispered his butty's name over and over, Emil, Emil, not as if to find him but to mourn him already because he knew

Štefan, John Chibala said

Here, Johnny, Štefan said

Matty, John Chibala said

a cough and a groan and a voice sucking air

Here, John, Matty said

Ondro, John Chibala said

not to me, though, to the others, his voice resigned because he knew where I was standing just before the collapse, and any good miner would have known no man or boy could survive a collapse like that

I'm here, I said

I see you now, Ondro, with the help of God I see you, son, John Chibala said

and I wanted to tell him he saw me because I had to be here, because I followed him into the room when I could just as easily have gotten out, and that Wicked too had tried to follow, but I could see in the light of the carbide and its reflection in the dust that no one else was moving

Can you get to Emil back there, Štefan, John Chibala said

and I knew that Štefan was hurt because I could see in the light that he was bent as he worked with one hand to light his own lamp but could not and straightened his back and remained on his knees

Ondro, help him if you can, John Chibala said

and I wondered why John Chibala didn't move himself, but I crawled toward Štefan Bozak, though he was no more than a few feet away and his left arm dangled at his side, his jacket dark with blood at the shoulder, the dust settling on it and staying there like flour in the bottom of a greased baking pan, and yet he had a smile on him, or he forced a smile when I came through the light, though it appears to me now as a grimace when I think of what pain he must have been in, and he angled his head toward the part of the collapsed room where we both knew Emil lay, as if to say, This way, and we crawled over shards of stone and anthracite toward where, in the farthest reach of John Chibala's lamp, we could see Emil pressed to the ground with the entire ceiling of the back room on top of him, that ICC-14 box of dynamite pushed toward us, and I stopped speaking there on the porch and looked at the boy named Emil and his empty glass of lemonade, and I looked at his father, who seemed to wonder why it was I would not go on

Emil, I think there is more lemonade in the refrigerator and some fresh baked cookies in the bread box next to the stove, they're yours if you would like them, I said

and the boy stood quickly, picked up his empty

glass, and walked from the porch back into the house, and I told the older man, who was son to the butty named Emil, and the younger man, who had never known work in the mines, that although Emil was alive that day there was little we could do in the thin light of John Chibala's carbide and with what little strength Štefan Bozak had to get him out from under the pile of rock that was crushing him

Crushing, the older man said

Yes, I said

and I told him all that was visible of his father were his hands as they protruded from the rock that covered him, and his head, which was not entirely uncovered, but which had been hit so hard that one of his eyes was nearly gouged out and his teeth looked separated from his jaw, and Štefan Bozak knelt over him and with his one good arm stroked gently a portion of the man's head that was not bloodied, and he said again, Emil, Emil

Your father's last words were, I love her, Matty, I said

and I told them that from the light of the carbide I could see Emil's breath seem to push his teeth farther from his jaw, and Štefan bent over and kissed his head and touched his eyelids closed and whispered, God rest your soul, and Štefan looked at me and the box of ICC-14 dynamite at his feet and opened it with his good arm, and there were three blasting caps left in there, not worth saving on that day or any day, then he closed the lid and pushed the box away from him until it bumped up against the new wall of rock there in the dark, and that ICC-14 box of American Cyanamid dynamite with three blasting caps left in it rests next to the dust and bones of Emil Milenec still

IV

AND THE HEAT OF MIDDAY IN LATE AUGUST HERE IS a worn and weakening heat, the sun already tilting south so that it is shaded sooner by the red oaks in the forest that surrounds the house, and I have been repairing a stone wall that fell into disrepair last winter, but have only found the time to work on it now because the sawyer to whom I sold some of the timber in the forest has had to put me off for another week and won't be along today, so I have replaced a course of face stones on the wall and picked some carrots from my garden and come inside to heat what's left of a barley and mushroom soup I made yesterday for my lunch, a soup I learned how to make by watching my mother in the kitchen of the house in the patch, and all of this has me thinking about how my mother took me from the patch not long after the collapse, because the pain of mourning in those cold houses was so raw and bitter that some families were suspicious of me, and others held a grudge against me for being alive, and others held their suspicions and grudges against my mother for not wanting to be them, not wanting to be of them, and I found this resentment a darkness deeper than any tomb in the mines, and when we did leave, their suspicions and grudges were confirmed, though not to all, not to the priest, not to the butty Emil's pregnant girlfriend, who never married and never hid and never apologized for her sin of having a child out of wedlock when the man she loved was locked forever in a room underground, and not to Magda Chibala, the daughter of the miner John Chibala, a girl one year younger than I was, because I remember she didn't cry at the liturgy, though her mother sat in the front pew of St. Michael the Archangel church and sobbed in her grief, and after the service Magda came up to where I stood holding my hat tight in my hands and leaned in and hugged me, and her mother, who was close by, stopped crying and scowled and grabbed her by the arm and pulled her away, and Magda turned to look at me over her shoulder until my mother took me by the arm as well and we walked back to our house and made a light supper of barley and mushroom soup, and she told me over supper that we would be leaving as soon as the company paid, which would not be enough to change our station but would give us a chance to move to a place where others wouldn't know who we were, or where we were from, and, in the spring, the company did pay and they paid more than was required of them because the accident and the deaths of the miners and their butties, who were husbands and fathers and sons and friends, made The Daily Patriot in Harrisburg, The Washington Post, and the New York World, and the company wanted reporters who had begun to come to the patch to see that the already widowed mother of the mule boy was being shown compassion in the compassionless landscape of the Pennsylvania slag heaps, collieries, and coal towns, and a young John Lewis from the UMWA came to speak to the company men and the inside boss, but not to my mother or the other mothers and wives, though it didn't matter, because in June of that year we moved to a small house in Shenandoah on a street at the edge of town that was still close enough to town that my mother could walk to the shop where she had gotten a job as a seamstress and I could walk to school, and from sunup to sundown the Blue Mountain ridge stood still and distant in the front window of the house on that street, and I studied hard at school and read the books they gave me to read and figured the sums they gave me to figure, and I got into fights sometimes when other boys called me Mule Boy and asked me if I had to eat anyone down there in the dark, and I ignored them at first, but after a while I got tired of it and one day a boy asked me if I had touched the peckers of the dead men after they'd died

Or maybe before they died, he said

and a rage overcame me that day, because I didn't know why anyone would say such a thing, why anyone would even think such a thing, and I hit that boy so hard he went down and I bent over him and kept hitting him over and over until his face and my fists were covered with his blood, and when I was too tired to strike him anymore I stood up and walked home and washed my hands and opened my books, and I found out that night, when the father of the boy came to our house to ask why anyone would do such a thing, or even think to do such a thing, that I had broken his nose, his jaw, the bones of his face, and nearly knocked out his right eye

Like a whole team of mules had kicked him, the father said

and they had to send him up to the General Hospital in Wilkes-Barre to get everything set right, and my mother apologized for me, and when he asked her for money she closed the door, and I made my confession that Saturday with a priest I had never seen before, an old man who whispered in Latin and gave me the same penance I was given for taking the Lord's name in vain, and the other boys did not stop calling me Mule Boy, but never to my face after that, and when I saw that boy in school again, saw the cuts and scars and bruises he'd carry for the rest of his life, his face looked to me like the face of the dead butty Emil, and I made a vow to myself that I would not return anger or violence with anger and violence ever again, because I had seen how weak the flesh and bones of men and beast are when they are pressed hard against anything unforgiving, and I kept to myself and worked at school, and when it came time to graduate I applied to Bucknell Junior College to study engineering, and in the fall I left my mother in that house down in Shenandoah and went up to Wilkes-Barre and took a room in an old walk-up on the river by the General Hospital and rode the trolley down to school on the days I had class, and when my classes were done I walked over to the Gibbons brewery and stacked cases of beer for the trucks to deliver, and I didn't get paid much, but it was work and it was enough and I could get a little sleep and go to classes in the morning and stay for lab in the afternoon if I had to, the brewery would cover for me until five o'clock, and I liked the courses on Systems and Structures and I tolerated the Applied Mathematics, but the only class I loved and never wanted to miss was Professor Elias Gray's class on Shakespeare, because Shakespeare and Professor Gray both seemed out of place in that college of engineering, and yet there they were, writing of and speaking of tragedy, ambition, love, and the struggle Professor Gray said the old Greeks called the agon, which the word agony came from, and I pored over those plays in order to find out what Shakespeare knew of how men died, and then it was summer and I worked full-time at the brewery until school started again in the fall and

I went back, and things changed for me, a change I neither desired nor was ready for, the workload of engineering studies was more deadening than working in the mines, and I knew that Magda Chibala had begun classes at College Misericordia in the Back Mountain because she had written to me in the summer, telling me that she was entering the college run by the Religious Sisters of Mercy in Dallas, Pennsylvania, and when fall came she wrote to me again and invited me to visit her at school if I could find the time, since I was only a bus ride away from the Back Mountain, and I did, and that September and October and November I found myself doing not much more than working at the brewery and waiting to visit Magda on Saturdays, until I stopped going to classes altogether that semester, and on Christmas Eve I took the train down the line to Shenandoah to my mother's house and knocked the snow from my shoes and walked in through the door of the house and felt the warmth of the stove and smelled the soup and bread she was making for the Velija feast that night, and I placed the fish I had brought for the feast from the fishmonger on Market Street in Wilkes-Barre in the sink and she came out of her bedroom, where she had been reading, and we embraced and she greeted me with the holy kiss, and we sat together at the table in the kitchen, where we always sat together mornings before I went to school and evenings for supper and where I remained to do my schoolwork, and she put a pot of chamomile tea on the table and a fresh baked loaf of bread that had already come out of the oven and told me about things she never wrote of in her letters to me at school, the autumn there in Shenandoah, the work she did now at the church with widows and young mothers, the way in which she found that if she simply sat and listened to those women, simply said nothing at all except an initial, Tell me how you are today, they would begin to speak of things they wouldn't tell the priest, and she felt as though she was being called to listen to those women, to listen to their stories and their loss and their wanting still to be women in the wake of that loss, wanting to love and be loved, not just by God and their children but by another who would love them for the women they were, many of them still so young, and she turned to look out of the window of the kitchen, the window from which I used to look at the Blue Mountain hills every morning before I went to school and every evening when I came home and sat to do my schoolwork, and I said nothing to her and we were both quiet for a long time, until she asked me if I had heard from Magda Chibala, and I told her I had and that I had even gone up to Misericordia on the bus from Wilkes-Barre to visit her

More than once, I presume, she said

and I said yes and she raised her eyebrows and

I told her that Magda Chibala had written to me in the summer from Inkerman and invited me to visit her at the college, since we would be close, but I didn't go, not then

She wrote to me and asked for your address, my mother said

and I nodded and looked out at the Blue Mountain hills

Well, she wrote to me again from the college, and I decided I would like to visit her, I said

Yes, why not, she's lost so much, my mother said

and I didn't say anything else and my mother stood

We should get ready for dinner, she said

and she walked into the kitchen and gave the soup on the stove a stir and went to the sink and unwrapped and rinsed the fish I had brought from the monger on Market Street in Wilkes-Barre, and I opened white wine I had also brought for the Velija feast, along with some bottles of beer and a bottle of šlivovitz, and we drank and cooked that evening and spoke only of the weather and that seemed conversation enough, and we went to Mass at midnight for the Christmas Eve Vigil and woke the next day and fired the stove and went back to church for the Mass of Christmas Day and went home and had a breakfast of sausage and eggs and coffee, and I was able to sneak what little šlivovitz there was left over into my coffee, and I gave my mother a simple silver necklace with a cross on it for a gift, and she gave me a new Underwood typewriter with a gray metal casing and green keys, which surprised me, and she told me it was because I had been doing so well in school and she knew that often students from Bucknell Junior went on to study at Bucknell University, and sometimes to the University of Pennsylvania, and she thought for sure I could go wherever I wanted to go to study whatever I wanted to study, and I thanked her and placed the heavy Underwood typewriter on the kitchen table and rolled a piece of paper into it and sat down and thought about what I might type, then tapped out a line from King Lear I had remembered from Professor Gray's class, Howl, howl, howl, howl! O, you are men of stones, and the words moved beautifully over the page and I typed two more lines, Had I your tongues and eyes, I'd use them so / That heaven's vault should crack, and I stopped there and looked up to see my mother smiling, she who had never read King Lear and so would not know what came next, and she walked around to the back of my chair and read what I had typed, and the smile left her

I don't know what that means, she said

and I told her I had done poorly at school in all but one class and, though I would be returning to Wilkes-Barre in a few days to finish my exams for the semester, I wasn't going back to school for the next semester because they wouldn't have me back,

I was going back to work at the brewery because it was a job and the boss had promoted me to driver and it paid my bills, and in the spring I could figure out where to go and what to do next, and I remember thinking, I abjure all roofs, and I could see she was trying not to cry

Oh Ondro, I thought this was what you wanted, she said

and she shook her head and lowered it and touched the cross hanging around her neck, and I didn't know what I wanted

It's Magda Chibala, she's why you want to leave school, she said

and I didn't say yes or no, I didn't say anything

You have to leave school and go to work because of her, don't you, don't you tell me there's a baby, she said

There is no baby, I said

and she turned and walked into the kitchen and nothing and everything changed, just as it had all those years later on that day in August when the son and grandson and great-grandson of the butty Emil showed up at my guard booth on my last day of work to find out how their father and grandfather and great-grandfather had died, if he had suffered, what his last words were, and we went back to my house on the pond in the shadow of the old mountain in New Hampshire and I told them, and afterward I insisted they stay the night and in the morning made coffee and cooked breakfast for them on the stove and gave them a gallon jug of cold springwater for the radiator of the Plymouth, and as they drove away the boy named Emil kept looking out the window at me, his hand up, not waving, just suspended there, as if in the air, he who resembled his father so much, and his father so much his father, and it was as if time had folded over on itself and the butty Emil was everywhere in that car, driver, passenger, boy in the backseat not waving but watching someone, something, as if we had finished that day in January 1929 and gone up top and gotten our pay and kept working through the Depression and the start of the war I would not go to, and the butty Emil kept working and got married and became a miner and raised a son who grew up and never once went down into the mines, and neither did his grandson nor his great-grandson, not anyone anymore, and I turned away and walked back into my house, knowing there was one more out there who would come to hear the story about which she had always longed to hear, whether she knew what that longing was or not, and I didn't do much work that day, it was hot, so I stayed down by the water and fished for perch in the afternoon and caught a few and cooked them on a small fire and slept out under the stars, the ghosts quiet, the loons just loons ululating over the water, the night with a certain peace to it, and the next day I walked back up the hill to the house and fired my stove, made my coffee, and took the sheaf of papers Jacobson had given to me when I left prison with Jonah written in Hebrew in bold pencil on the first page, and I sat down in the chair on the porch beneath the old white pine and read the story of the prophet, as I have done every year on this day, and have done since I came to the mountain, read of the prophet told to rise and speak of God's anger, but who flees instead, flees onto a ship, where a storm follows, until the fear and anger and realization of the sailors tosses Jonah into the sea, where he is eaten by a fish and spit out on the shores of Nineveh, and so he crosses the vast city and speaks of God's anger, and the Ninevites repent and believe, as though they have come from darkness into a light, and they cover themselves with sackcloth and ashes, a feeling on the body I know, a feeling every miner with a coal stove knew, a feeling every miner's child whose job it was to empty those ashes from the stove knew as well, the weight of them, the burned-off sulfur smell of them, the scratch of cinders to the arms and body when they got inside your clothes and worked their way along the waist and back after you had dumped them on the ash heap, yes, every miner and miner's child knew this ancient feeling of repentance as surely as they knew the need to keep warm, but Jonah is unable to understand or recognize this repentance, and so he sits beneath the shade of a tree that understands the ways of God better than he does, or so it seems, and Jonah must be taught with questions, as though a child, taught about God's mercy and magnanimity, which aren't meant to be questions, but reminders of mercy and magnanimity, and that was what I was reading beneath the shade of my own tree that day, the story Jacobson taught me to read and then gave to me written out in Hebrew with his smuggled and worn-down pencils on eight pages of paper in slightly oversized script so that I could read it better, eight pages I keep in a wooden box I made and place on the bookshelf where my Collected Shakespeare and all of the books I've acquired over the years rest, when I needed in those days to put more than the memory of being in that mine in front of me, needed to be reminded of mercy and magnanimity, because two years later, strangely on the same day in August the son, grandson, and great-grandson of the butty Emil Milenec had come to me in their Plymouth, I looked out across the field that faced the mountain and saw two women walking up the long drive from the dirt road, one young and carrying two suitcases, the other older, though no slower, and I stood and put the sheaf of papers on which Jacobson had transcribed the book of Jonah in Hebrew in the box I had built for them and placed the box on the floor of the porch and walked across the grass and down the path and took both suitcases from the young woman, and I knew who they were, because I remembered the face of the older woman from the patch, though she was much younger then, and I could see the butty Matty in the face of his daughter

It's been a long time, Hortensia, I said

It has, Ondro, she said

Come in, I'll put tea on, I said

and both women followed me into the house, where I placed their suitcases down by the door and walked over to the kitchen table, pulled two chairs out and asked them if they would like to sit and rest after their journey, which they did, then I went to the stove and moved the kettle full of water to the front of the stove and got out the teapot and a tin of Irish tea one of the rangers at the state park still brought me every month from the store in Harrisville and sat back down at the table

So, this is where you ran off to, Hortensia said

Yes, but the running came to an end a long time ago, I said

Did it, she said.

and I didn't say anything, not knowing if she meant it to be a question or not

You look well, she said

As do you, I said

and she cocked her head toward her daughter, who I knew was named Nela

You remember when she was a baby, Hortensia said

and it was not a question, and I nodded and held out my hand to the young woman

Welcome, Nela, I said

Thank you, Mr. Prach, she said

Call me Ondro, I was barely older than you are now when I left, I said

and we were all three quiet until the water on the stove began to boil, and I excused myself and stood and walked to the counter and placed three scoops of the Irish tea into the pot and went over to the stove and took the kettle off the heat and poured it over the leaves in the pot, gave it a stir with a spoon, put the lid on, took three cups and saucers from the cupboard and placed them on the table, then went back to the tea and brought it over and poured it through a strainer into each cup and sat back down

You stayed at the hotel last night, I said

How did you know, Hortensia said

There's nowhere else you could have spent the night, except in a tent, and you don't have a tent, I said

The man from the hotel drove us to the bottom of your path but didn't want to drive us all the way to your door, she said

and I sipped my tea and waited for one or the other to speak again, but I knew why and for what they had come, or rather why Nela had come, because Hortensia would have believed she knew all she cared to know about the day her husband died, but not her daughter, who might have remembered vague outlines of her father, the image of his face and maybe the echo of a laugh, but not much beyond that, and so she was the one for whom I waited, and it was she about whom Hortensia began to speak

Nela, you know, has been asking about him ever since she was a girl, and here she is a grown woman and she still asks about him, and then I heard from Tommy Milenec that he and his son and grandson had come here to see you, and to talk to you, and he told me it wasn't no picnic getting to this place, and listening to you talk about his father wasn't one either, but he got what he wanted, so I looked at a map and at Christmas promised Nela that when summer came and we could travel we would take the train to Boston and then out to Fitchburg and find a way to get to here from there, she said

They were here exactly two years ago to the day, I said

Yes, she said

I don't get many visitors, I said

I can't understand why, she said

and she smiled and looked at her daughter, who smiled too and looked down at the table as though embarrassed by the realization that she was the reason they had come this far, spent money on train tickets and hotel rooms and had carried their leather suitcases all the way to the door of Ondro Prach's house, the mule boy, and the young woman looked at me as if it was her turn to explain not how but why they had come

My daughter just turned sixteen last fall, Mr. Prach, she's so bright and lovely and she wants to go to college, and we live in Glen Lyon, you know, not far from an old breaker and the culm banks, and she sees photos of the old days in our house and asks all the time about Grandpa and other men and what it was like in that time, as though we live in another country when some of those men are still alive, though not many, and she has a way about her, an old soul, I once heard my mother call her, she said

and she blushed a little and looked over at her mother, but Hortensia was looking down into her tea, listening, and Nela turned back to me

And so I thought maybe I should come and find out what Tommy Milenec found out, maybe there's a story I need to tell my daughter about the men in the photos, because we visit the graves of her aunts and uncles, and when we come home, my old soul, my little one, always asks where her grandfather's grave is, Nela said

And of course she can't answer her, and I can't answer her either, Hortensia said

and Nela looked down into her tea, though she had the hint of a smile on her face, a wistful one, as though she were thinking about her little girl, her old soul, and this gave her some pleasure in the moment

No, we can't, but she's a smart girl, and she'll go away to college next year and I'll lose her, so maybe if I had an answer for her, or found an answer for her, we could share that and she wouldn't feel as though her family was so far away then, Nela said

and I listened as she spoke and sipped my tea until they were both silent and I thought they might want me to say something

It's the children who want to know because they haven't felt the loss, haven't tried to live with it, only known life without it, I said

Yes, it's the children, Nela said

and I could feel them looking at me, waiting for me, and I put my hands flat on the surface of the table and felt the wood with the pads of my fingertips and the flesh of my palms and thought about how soft both were because I could feel the coarse surface of the wood out of which I had made my table, and I remembered that when I worked in the mines as a boy I used to stare at my hands as though they were somehow separate from my body, nothing hurt them, nothing could hurt them, they were so calloused and hardened because I never wore gloves, not because my mother couldn't afford them but because the miners and their butties never wore gloves, the one thing they could have spent their money on and did not, because they didn't need them once their hands were calloused harder than any pair of gloves could ever be, even good leather ones, and I looked up at Hortensia and Nela, daughter of the butty Matty, and I told them about the morning and the cage and robbing the pillars on breast number seven and the moments of the collapse, just as I had told the son and grandson and great-grandson of the butty Emil, and then I told them they had to understand there was no day or night down there, there was only light and no light and that depended on how much carbide one could or wanted to burn in order for there to be light, and after the miner Štefan Bozak and I knelt in front of the half-crushed body of the butty Emil and watched him breathe his last by the light of a carbide, I heard John Chibala move and groan, knowing we had just watched the butty Emil die

We should save the wicks, we won't need light to figure our way out of this, not yet anyway, John Chibala said

and Štefan Bozak extinguished his lamp and we all sat right where we were without moving in the dark, dark so thick you could not see the hand in front of your face, could not feel the hand brought to your face, as though the dark's thickness were a barrier to touch, but you could hear in the dark, you could hear almost everything that made a sound, and we all sat there and listened to the dust settle with an intermittent hiss that made me wonder if more rock would come down, and then I thought of gas, black damp, the killer no miner could see or smell, only detect with his lamp, and, as though he knew what I was thinking, though more likely because I had twitched quickly with the thought, John Chibala moved in his place at the other side of the room and again I could hear him groan

We'd be dead from it by now, Ondro, ňestaraj śe, he said

and he asked the miner Štefan Bozak if it was an explosion or a collapse and Štefan said he was certain it was a collapse, the ceiling weakened, he believed, by the work being done in a breast above, where there wasn't supposed to be a breast above, and we were lucky to have had this section fall just so around us, though Emil was not so lucky, if only he hadn't thought to go back for that damn box, but he knew not to waste anything, not to leave it, he'd need it again or have to pay for it at the store, and Štefan Bozak cursed and John Chibala told him they needed to figure how to get dug out or how to get a message up to someone who could do the digging from the other side, and he asked Štefan if he was all right, if he could move, and Štefan said yes but his side hurt, hurt badly when he breathed, and John Chibala asked me the same and I told him I didn't feel anything that hurt or was broken, and although the dust was making me cough a bit and my eyes stung, I could do everything except stand in that room because the ceiling was barely four feet above us, and John Chibala called over to his butty Matty again, but Matty didn't answer this time, and John Chibala asked Štefan Bozak if he could light his lamp, so Štefan blew the falling dust out of the burner and lit the lamp, and I could see then that John Chibala was sitting up with his legs pinned and Matty was nearly across from him, sitting too but with a strange vacancy to his eyes, so I crawled over to him and touched his shoulder and he winced and tried to raise his hand, and as he did the hand dangled by one thread of muscle from the wrist and there was a lot of blood all of a sudden, and Štefan Bozak leaped so fast I thought he would crash into the two of us there in that room, but he pulled his shirt off and made a sound like a roar as he did and tore a long strip from it, and in the light of his own carbide he had me hold the butty Matty's arm out and just as quickly tied the shirt into a tourniquet around the arm, and the bleeding stopped, and I placed the arm back down at Matty's side and he never said a word, he just stared ahead into the wall of anthracite in front of him lit up by Štefan Bozak's carbide lamp, and there was so much blood I could feel it now on the floor of the mine where I was kneeling, still warm, and Štefan moved away and I heard the sound of tin scraping on the rock floor, and when his lamp light came back into view he had his growler bucket and he moved beside me and held the bucket up to Matty's lips and Matty drank, and I could smell the beer, the yeast and honey smell that Štefan Bozak's house always smelled of, and no one ever called the authorities on him because they knew the beer, Štefan, and that smell would go away if they did, and Matty seemed to come back to life then and took a deep breath and let out a long low wail and opened his eyes

It hurts like hell, Štefan, he said

and I looked down at the butty Matty's hand in the light of Štefan Bozak's carbide and it was white, all white, and hung from the stump of bone and veins like a cut of meat in the butcher shop in the town outside the patch, and I could see the dust and blue marks on the bone where there was no blood and it was clear his hand had been cut by a falling slab of anthracite, but the arm above the tourniquet had some color to it again, and I knew we had caught him just in time and the butty Matty might not bleed to death there in that room if we could get out, and Štefan Bozak gave him another sip of beer and he breathed deep for the pain and then his breathing leveled out, like a man who knew he had a hard task ahead, and he asked about Emil, and John Chibala and Štefan Bozak looked at each other as if for direction there in the brightness of the carbide light

Tell me, Štefan, Matty said

Emil's with God, Štefan said

and the butty Matty let out the breath he had been holding in with the same long low wail, the breath of a man who is all at once resting in order to fight and resigned to accepting defeat

Is this where it ends, Matty said

I don't know, Matty, I don't know, but I promised you we'd be up top before the shift buzzer and, unless this is Hell and we're already dead, I'm a man who keeps a promise, John Chibala said

and the butty Matty managed a small laugh and winced and Štefan Bozak put his head up and surveyed the room with his carbide so that John Chibala could see what he was doing and followed the beam of the carbide as it swept the collapse that surrounded us from top to bottom, and we could all see now where we were, the ten-wide and four-high cell that encased us, the butty Emil resting facedown under a blanket of rock farthest back in the room

We're in here real good, Johnny, Štefan Bozak said

Save the light, John Chibala said

and Štefan Bozak turned the wick of the carbide down and the light in that cell felt to me as though it was being sucked through some unseen fissure in those walls until all around us there was once again nothing but dark, a dark so thick you could breathe it, and we all sat quiet in that dark, and I could smell the beer the butty Matty had just drunk, and I could smell lunch on the breaths of John Chibala and Štefan Bozak in the closeness of the cell, and I knew they could smell me too, and we sat in the dark and waited

I didn't kiss my Nela this morning, Matty said

and I could hear in his voice that he was breathing fast

I had already put my hat and this filthy coat on and was out on the road, but I ran back to the house and opened the door and Hortensia scolded me because she had just cleaned the day before, We don't live on a farm, Matty, and I laughed because she was always talking about moving to a place where we could see grass instead of slag and so I kissed her again, but not my Nela, he said

and he sounded winded speaking those words, his breath quickening as he tried to pull the air from that room into his chest so that he could speak just those words, and then he began to sob, though it sounded at first like a cough that turned into a sob, resigned and regretful

Matty, John Chibala said

Matty, ňestaraj śe, you'll see her again, there's air coming in from somewhere, he said

and there in the dark John Chibala and Štefan Bozak made a plan to use what light there was to search the rubble at the entrance and find out where an opening was, if there was one, but John

Chibala couldn't move and Štefan Bozak was getting winded quickly when he did, and it fell to me to find the place where the rock was loose and pull it away so that I could crawl out and find what rescuers would be searching for us, because they would be searching for us

It's not that, Matty said

and his breathing slowed as he said this

I wanted to tell Emil too, I needed to tell him, but who thinks this is the day his friend will die, he said

Tell him what, John Chibala said

His girl, his angel, I tried to steal a kiss from her behind the store, Matty said

and now Hortensia looked up from her tea and Nela stopped drinking hers, and I knew I was at a place where I could not stop, a place from which I could never return, because we were in my home and they had come so far to hear this from me, but still I wondered if they knew the difference between want and need

I know you have come a long way, but I can stop if it's best, I said

and they looked at each other, mother and daughter, and Hortensia turned back to me

Go on, she said

and I told them that, out of a wild delirium and fear almost, crying like a child who had lost his mother or his best friend, Matty confessed to us that he and his wife had to get married because he had gotten her with child, and he loved her, yes, but she was not a beauty, not an angel, and Emil's girl was such an angel, and just once he thought, Why can't I have the angel, and that's why he tried to kiss her

But she didn't let me, she didn't let me, Emil, Matty said

and he tried to turn his head to speak in the direction of where his dead friend lay in the corner of breast number seven and began sobbing again, so loudly that we thought for sure someone outside could hear him, and then he stopped and took a deep breath of what air there was in there

Johnny, I wish I could see them, Matty said

and he began to sob again, loud and mournful and uncontrolled, and even in the dark we could tell he was shaking along the entire length of his body from the sounds he made

I wish I could see them both again, my Nela and my Hortensia, he said

You'll see them again, Matty, ňestaraj śe, John Chibala said

and he stopped as quickly as he began and drew breath in a heave

I don't know, Johnny, the pain in my arm, I can't bear it and I want to sleep, just go to sleep, but I want to see them, I want to kiss Nela again and tell Hortensia that I love her, that I've always loved her, that I always have, Matty said

and his voice trailed off then

Matty, John Chibala said

but Matty didn't reply, and John Chibala must have thought Matty had gone to sleep and so he asked me if I was ready to move some rock and I told him I was, and he said we should give it ten minutes of good searching and I should move only those rocks I could move myself and to be careful to look at what was resting on top of anything I thought could move, because heavy on top of loose meant a slide and more collapse, and I told him I understood, and Štefan Bozak lit his carbide lamp and the room brightened as if the sun had risen for us underground, and we all three at once looked over at the butty Matty, who lay there whitened like the Holy Ghost, his head lolled against the rock wall, his chest still, his good arm in his lap, the other hanging limp and lifeless inside the coat sleeve at his side

God rest your soul, Matty, God rest your soul, Štefan Bozak said

and John Chibala looked away and took a breath that I could see pained him

We don't have much time with the light, Ondro, dig now, he said

and I moved toward where there was once the opening of a breast mined for coal and was now a rock pile that sealed us in a room where two men had already died and the other two and a boy wondered when their time would come, and I knelt down and began to pull at the slabs of stone and shale and coal as though to save the others, as though it were for them I could move and breathe and raise my arms, and when I looked across the table at Nela and Hortensia Holub in my house there in the shadow of the mountain in New Hampshire, Hortensia was weeping and Nela had her arm around her mother, holding her like no one had for all these years

V

AND TODAY, AFTER I HAVE FINISHED THE STONE wall and a lunch of leftover barley and mushroom soup and my reading of the prophet Jonah in Hebrew, I go down to the water to row my boat, and I row out to the middle of the pond, where the summit of the mountain is visible, and I ship my oars and float on the windless surface, and for a moment I think that I will strip down and jump into the water because it's warm this afternoon and I am floating in a place where I know there are springs of cold water, which flow down from the mountain and push up from the bottom of the pond, but it's difficult for me to climb back into the boat these days, and so I lean against the stern and stare at the blue sky and the summit of the mountain in the distance, where I can see a storm coming, and I think of something Jacobson said to me in prison once, that the path my life took was the only path it could have taken, a path that put me on a path to intersect his, the man who taught me enough Hebrew to know how to read the one book he thought I should know in Hebrew, the man who taught me how to play chess and study geometry and understand something of what the ancients believed, the man who told the other prisoners that I was madness incarnate and taught me how to smuggle books and paper and pencils past the guards, though I knew nothing of where or from whom to get those things on the outside, the man with whom I read Plutarch and Maimonides and Shakespeare out loud, the man they would not let into a university to study Greek and literature and mathematics with other men because he did not believe in what those other men believed, had not lived the way they lived, no, and I remember thinking that, even before my mother and I moved from the patch to Shenandoah, all of the newspapers in Nanticoke, Hazelton, and Wilkes-Barre had begun to call the cave-in the New Year's Mine Disaster, and they wrote about it and gave the names of the miners and their butties, but no one mentioned the mule boy, and I think that was what made her want to move from the patch, to get out of her prison, as she said later, because she used to say, If they wish you had died, then let's give them nothing to look at, so, yes, that was when she started searching for a way out of the patch, but I can't say I wanted to go, because it's not true everyone wished I had died, Magda Chibala was glad I was alive, I was certain of it, because even after she embraced me at the liturgy, she often waited at the corner of the schoolhouse at the end of the day when she knew I would be on my way to the store for my mother, and she would raise her head when I caught her eye and I could see her thick black hair rumpled and wispy and wild from the wind that blew through the patch no matter the season, even though she had tried to tie it back, and although she wasn't smiling, her face with those gray eyes that seemed to sit like platinum orbs above her cheekbones bore some kind of deific image, as though a sadness and a peace came to rest together in one place, and she would raise her head and stand up straighter when she saw me coming, as if to say she wanted to speak to me, but I would not speak to her, I could not speak to her, out of the fear in me of everyone in the patch, especially those who were family to the miners and butties, and at Mass when my mother and I walked up from the back of the church for Communion and Magda Chibala was in the front pew with her mother, I knew she watched me from the moment I appeared in her peripheral vision to when I took Communion and walked back to our pew away from the rest of the congregation, and once at the beginning of Advent, when my mother had come back from the store herself because I was sick in bed with a touch of the flu, she told me as she heated the soup and cooked the noodles she had bought along with bread and tea at the store that John Chibala's daughter, Magda, had spoken to her and asked how I was, because she knew it was I who always went to the store, and my mother told her I was home with the grippe but it didn't seem serious and she promised she would mention that Magda Chibala was asking after me, and I didn't say anything to my mother, so she went about cooking the noodles she had bought to put in my soup and slicing the loaf of bread, which she slathered with margarine and grape jam she kept in a small larder, and neither one of us spoke of the girl again, but I knew she was glad I was alive, and Magda and her mother moved out of the patch up the line to Inkerman a month before my mother and I moved to Shenandoah and I stopped wondering about her, stopped thinking about her entirely as I went from ignored to embattled and showed those who came at me that their anger and meanness were nothing compared to what lay deep in my own heart, and then my vow to leave that hurt buried there rather than to turn their anger and meanness back onto them, and this brought me my first peace, the better fight, one I would hold on to the longest, and it was for this reason I was surprised when Magda Chibala wrote to me at Bucknell Junior College from Inkerman and told me that she would be going to school at College Misericordia on a full scholarship the owners of the mine had cobbled together for her because she was the only child of the miners who wanted to go to college, and she said in the letter that she was excited because they had accepted her to study biology and science, and even though she didn't want to leave her mother, who was no better and no worse these days, an old aunt had agreed to move in and live with and take care of the woman in her silence and grief, and that seemed like the best thing to do, even the old aunt said, because there was no use ruining the lives of two women when one of those women stood to do some good in the world, and it wasn't far to go from the Back Mountain to Inkerman by bus or train, and she said she wrote to my mother to ask for my address and permission to write to me and my mother granted both, so she was writing to tell me that she would be starting a new life of sorts in the fall and she hoped I was doing well at Bucknell Junior in the city, and maybe I could take the trolley up to Inkerman one day in the summer before she left for school and pay a visit, if I had time away from my studies, or work, if it was work I did to pass the summers, before she had to move, and I folded the letter up and placed it back in the envelope and left it on the small table in my apartment and put a can of beans on the hot plate and took out of my coat pocket the bottle of beer I had helped myself to from a case I saw sitting on the edge of the delivery truck when my shift was over, and I cracked open the beer and took a swig and sat down in the only chair I had at that table and looked at the river from the filthy window of my apartment, looked out at the mountains to the west, and I wished Magda well up there at the all-girls school on the hill, but there was no question she would do well, no question at all, and she did, studying biology as a major because she wanted to go to medical school, and she even worked for a Religious Sister of Mercy who had made something of a name for herself as a writer, worked as her secretary and put her initials, MC, at the end of the essays she transcribed for the religious woman, until the science department heard about this and threatened to take away Magda's scholarship, so she kept working for the sister but signed her mother's initials from her maiden name, IS, at the end of the essays and no one ever knew or found out, and she told me this when I went up to the Back Mountain from Wilkes-Barre one Saturday late in the fall when she was at school and had written me one more letter saying she was sorry I never got to see her in Inkerman during the summer, but it was probably just as well and would I come to visit her at the college, and I was in the same place in my apartment reading the letter, the same chair at the same table and looking out the filthy window at the river, then at the mountains to the west, and I could see her as I read, see her writing the letter and reading it out loud as she wrote, her wild black hair and eyes like platinum orbs, her graceful hand almost carving her sentences across the face of the letter with the ink that pooled slightly in the place where she began to write again after dipping it in her inkwell, and I felt a longing for her because I hadn't stopped thinking about her, wondering about her, and I felt as though, if I didn't see her again, I would wander through the world alone and empty and looking for her my whole life, and for a moment I was plunged back into the dark emptiness of that room in which I had been trapped with the miners and their butties, and I didn't want to be alone and empty, so I got a pen and tore off the bottom half of my paycheck, where there was always a blank and perforated section, and wrote that I would take the 8:00 A.M. bus from the square to the Back Mountain next Saturday and meet her at the porter's desk, and I mailed it and waited all week and got up early on Saturday morning and walked over to the square and got on the 8:00 A.M. bus and got off at the bank on Main Street in downtown Dallas and walked up Lake Street to the college, walked through the gateway arch and onto campus and walked up the steps of the small clapboard gatehouse where the porter sat, and he called over to Magda's dormitory and I waited and stared out of a small four-paned window in that house at a building in the distance and watched as Magda Chibala emerged from that building and walked toward the house in which I stood next to the porter's desk, and it was strange watching her move across the deep green lawn beneath towering deciduous beech and maple burning orange and red in the autumn air and onto a redbrick walkway that led right to the steps of the house in which I stood, she was older and more beautiful now and I felt an ache as she came toward me, and I wanted to leave because I didn't want to disturb her in this place that seemed so much like the home she should have, should always have, should always have had, and I was overcome with a fear that our meeting there would change the course of both our lives, a change that would not be the best for her, and yet I didn't leave, I was forced and frozen by some desire I knew and couldn't know, and then the door opened and she was standing in front of me, her face radiant, her black hair longer and still wild and windblown, and we didn't know if we should shake hands or embrace or just stand in front of each other like children who never knew what it was like to be children, until she leaned into me and gave me a kiss on the cheek

Thank you for coming, Ondro, she said

and I heard her father's voice in her voice, as though we were back there in the room in the dark, and I reached out and embraced her and we remained in that embrace until the porter cleared his throat with some volume and reminded us she had to sign out if she was going to leave campus, and so she signed out and we walked down the long redbrick path that led back through the gateway arch and out to Lake Street and into downtown Dallas, where we sat at a booth in a diner and drank coffee and ate apple pie and talked of where we'd been and where we thought we'd like yet to go after college and how odd it was even to think that we were in college, but we were, and she had an almost mystical focus on the future, one in which she knew she would study medicine and not just help her mother but help anyone who sought her help, and then she asked how my studies were and I told her they were about as creative as being inside a mine, then apologized, because I had seen how creative the men inside a mine could be, and she didn't say anything after that, and we walked back to campus and into a pine grove beneath the house where the old sisters lived and sat down on the grass in the autumn sun

You don't like it there in school, do you, she said

and I said I did not, but I would give it another semester, not knowing yet what I would tell my mother at Christmas

Yes, give it another semester, she said

and she told me we were lucky to have this chance to become someone other than a miner or the wife of a miner, and I said we'd always be the children of miners

We'll always be that, she said

and we stood and agreed that I would visit the next Saturday, and on the bus back to Wilkes-Barre and in my flat near the brewery I thought about whether I was in love with Magda Chibala, or if I felt guilty for the fact that her father died in that mine and I got out, and not just out of the mine but out of the mines and the patch and an entire world of people whose lives began and ended in the mines, and she too, though her mother sat in a house in Inkerman and stared at a wall all day, ignoring the aunt who cooked and cleaned up after her, stared at a wall as though she were in the mines herself and knew nothing of what her daughter was studying so she could find some way to reach her mother again, pull her out of that mine too, and I told myself it was love, but what could I do now that she was in a cloister on a hill in the Back Mountain and I was one semester away from dropping out of Bucknell Junior College, because I was less interested in studying engineering than I was in taking a job driving a beer truck up and down the line all day so that I could grab a few bottles from the odd case that teetered off the back of the truck and hit the ground and the bottles that didn't break were the ones I stashed in my coat pockets and under the seat, except when it was payday and I could afford to buy a whole case with the discount the brewery gave me, but I thought of Magda and nothing else all that week, then took the bus to the Back

Mountain the next Saturday, and I kept taking the bus to the Back Mountain from Wilkes-Barre to see her every Saturday in the fall because I wanted to see her as often as I could, and when she asked me once if I shouldn't be back at school studying, I told her I studied in the evening and didn't need much sleep, but I think she knew, without my having to tell her, that by Christmas college was over for me, and that's what I told her when I returned from my mother's house in Shenandoah after Christmas and Magda came down to Wilkes-Barre to pick up a book on the work of Emilie du Châtelet at the Osterhout Free Library and we met in the square and she told me she would have to work harder that semester to keep her scholarship, but we could see each other on breaks and in the summer because she planned to stay in the Back Mountain and work for Sister Bernadette, and so all that spring I worked and drank and typed letters to Magda on my new Underwood, sometimes two letters a day, one in the morning and one in the evening, not saying much with any insight or purpose, often just describing a pigeon that had landed on my window ledge, or re-creating sounds from the traffic on the street below with the letters I could type on the keys of my Underwood, but I was letting her know I was still here, still waiting, wanting her to know it was something I could do, and the sound of that typewriter in my flat was a consolation to me, like the intermittent drips of water from the roof of the room in which I was sealed with the miners John Chibala and Štefan Bozak after their butties Matty and Emil had breathed their last, water from the ceiling dripping with a soft and muffled tap tap tap that let us know we would not die of thirst, that we would have water to drink, and I remember sitting next to John Chibala in the dark while Štefan Bozak slept, and after a long silence through which I could hear only the water dripping, he turned to me

I will miss seeing what becomes of my Magda, he said

and then nothing else, as though he were alone in that room and had taken a break from work, and not one of us moved, not one of us spoke, even Štefan Bozak's wheezing breath seemed to have settled into what sleep he could get, and we were so quiet all we could hear was that slow tap tap tap of water dripping from the ceiling onto the floor like a clock we had forgotten hung on the stone wall of that breast

You hear that, Ondro, he said

and I wondered why John Chibala had only then heard the dripping, not heard it sooner, as I had

We're not sealed in, get a growler and catch the water, he said

and I did, and the clocklike tapping of the

water against the stone became like the dull and loud clanging of a bell against the bottom of the growler, a bell so loud it woke Štefan Bozak, and in the dark even I could tell he had startled and tried to move and took in a breath as if to holler from the pain and grabbed his side and hissed

That's a god-awful sound to wake up to, Johnny, he said

and we let that growler fill until there was enough water for each of us to have a good drink, cold and tasting a little of sulfur, but we knew it was good because we were a long way down underground, and during the spring term break of her second year, Magda asked me to come out to the Back Mountain on a Saturday, and we walked down into the center of Dallas and stopped for some food at the same café on Lake Street and she asked me if I had ever thought of trying to get a job and an apartment in the Back Mountain, and I said I had not, I liked my job at the brewery, the boss liked me, and I liked that I didn't have to pay for the beer I drank, sometimes as many as I wanted, and I probably shouldn't have been as honest as I was, but I had had a few beers already that day on the bus, and we didn't talk about much more after that, and I took the bus back into Wilkes-Barre in the afternoon and Magda finished her semester of classes that year, and in the summer I bought a car, a used 1928 Ford Model A, and I drove that car up to the college from Wilkes-Barre to see her on weekends and we would drive down into Fernbrook Park, or out to the Harvey's Lake Picnic Grounds, where we rode the roller coaster and ate doughnuts and cotton candy, and she told me that once when she was a little girl her father and mother took her from the patch to a fair in Hazelton and she had cotton candy there for the first time and loved it and always would because it reminded her of that day when she and her father and mother were just a family at the fair in Hazelton

You were there too, I remember I told you my name and we sat and talked and all you would ask me was if I really liked cotton candy, and I said yes, she said

I remember, I said

and at the end of the day I took her back to the college, where she signed in with the porter and said good night to me and gave me a kiss on the cheek, and I drove back to Wilkes-Barre and sat in my flat by the river and nursed a few beers, and sometimes a glass of Heaven Hill before I had to get up for work in the morning, and we did this for the next two years, until the spring she graduated from College Misericordia and the used car I had bought threw a rod on Highway 309 as I drove to her commencement that day, so I left it on the side of the road and hitched a ride to the college and got there just as she was lining up with the rest of the graduates on stage, and I watched her receive her diploma and look out to see if anybody else was there, anyone she might know who knew this was the day she was graduating from college, and I looked around too but didn't see anyone I knew or even recognized, until I realized she was looking for me, and so I stood there on the lawn of the college watching her, her eyes still platinum, her hair black and wild and windblown-looking even beneath her graduation cap, and I waved, and she saw me and seemed a little surprised, but I knew she had been looking for me, expecting me, and she waved back, and then one by one all of those women who had gotten their diplomas walked off the stage and into the arms of people who loved them, and Magda walked over to me and we didn't say anything, but she hugged me, and I took the diamond I had bought the week before from my pocket and on the lawn of College Misericordia asked Magda Chibala if she would be my wife, and we were married that July at Gate of Heaven church in Dallas and stayed that night at a house on Harvey's Lake that belonged to the father of a friend of hers, a rich friend, I gathered, because the place was large and built of stone and had a wraparound porch and was tucked back into the pines away from the road but had its own long stretch of lakefront, and we were all alone in that house, making love in the stultifying heat of our wedding day as though we had been waiting all our lives for that day, and we might have been, and the sun went down and evening cooled with a breeze off the lake, and in the morning there were eggs and milk and bread that her friend had left for us in the icebox, and I marveled at the generosity and magnanimity of such people, and we ate, then walked down to the lakefront and out onto the dock and sat in the warm sun next to the boathouse, where a varnished wood powerboat was tied off to cleats and bobbed there at its anchorage, as if waiting for the right people to come by, people who were not us, and when it got to the heat of the day, we took off our clothes and Magda saw the rosary in my pocket when I dropped my trousers on the dock and she picked it up and looked at me as if to ask where I had gotten it, and I told her the story of my father that my mother had told me, and she held the rosary in her hand and curled her fingers around the beads, and I thought, Now they have received you too, and she uncurled her fingers and placed the rosary back in the pocket of my trousers, and we jumped from the dock into the cold lake and swam, and it was as if I had come out of a torpor, the heat, the lovemaking, the beer I had put in the icebox next to the eggs and milk and bread and had been drinking all day, as if I had surfaced from the bottom of a deep lake after I had wondered if I would ever see anything other than dim lights in a fathomless dark again, or hear any voices other than men's voices at the edge of pain, and the sun was bright, so bright it hurt my eyes, and my body tingled from the shock of the cold, and Magda swam up next to me and into my arms so that the cold could not get between the heat that was our bodies pressed to each other, and I knew everything was different, everything was saved, every moment of the past had come to this and in doing so had disappeared in that moment, if only for a moment, and we went back to the house and made love again in the afternoon, then packed up and hitched a ride into Dallas, took the bus to Wilkes-Barre, and spent the night in my flat on River Street, where Magda seemed to sleep like a baby, but I stayed up all night and into the morning, listening to the growing traffic of cars barreling through the city, horns blasting when one was too close, a screech of brakes when the horn was not enough, and it felt to me like some ancient city that had just come to know the automobile, but knew the noise of impatience and speed and commerce nevertheless, the movement and bustle of it no different from the mines when hundreds of men worked to bring the goods of an ancient city underground to the modern cities up top, and I knew I could not live there much longer, and I wanted to wake Magda and tell her, but when I turned to look at her she looked like an angel in her attitude of sleep and I could not, could not wake her to tell her anything other than that I had loved her from the day I crawled out of that mine, and I knew that we would not be together much longer, because I worked the night shift at the brewery after I had been pulled from driving the truck for damaging a service bay and almost taking the leg off of one of the stockers who had come out to see why my truck was late, and Magda took a job in the laboratory of the General Hospital, running test tubes of blood and slides of tissue and things she would refer to as samples of cytopathology, as though that were even a word people used, and all that fall we ate dinner together after she had come from work and I was getting ready to leave, and we talked about where we might go once we got on our feet, but those were rare talks, because we didn't talk much, and she wondered out loud one day in late November, after we had been to my mother's in Shenandoah for Thanksgiving dinner, if the war in Europe was going to come here, and I said I didn't know, and honestly I didn't care, I had registered with the Selective Service at the post office in September and been given a number, and then I got on with my life, with work, where I lifted cases and loaded the trucks I used to drive, the night shift a thing I came to prefer for its quiet and lack of oversight, and in a way it was where I belonged, and Magda and I tried to have a child, and there was a time in the spring when her period was late, later than usual, and I remember because I went a whole weekend and into a Monday without having anything to drink, I was so focused with anticipation on what her being late might mean, though I trembled, and not from fear, and the day before Magda was scheduled to go in to the doctor's office for a test I came home after my shift to find her sitting in the kitchen with a cup of tea, just sitting quietly, and when I sat down next to her she told me she had gotten her period that night, and I put my arm around her and told her I loved her and that we would be fine, and the first glass of bourbon I drank that night felt to me like I had come up out of a mine, and I don't remember much more of what it felt like after that, and in the summer of 1941 we didn't go anywhere, not to Fernbrook Park, not to the Harvey's Lake Picnic Grounds, not even to the public beach for a swim, no, I worked the night shift and came home after Magda had gone to work herself, and I drank whiskey with my breakfast because it was dinnertime for me, and I drank a few more beers after that for a nightcap and went to sleep close to noon and slept in the heat of the flat and woke up just as she came home from work, and she wouldn't look at me unless I had a hard time getting out of bed and then she would just stand in the doorway of our bedroom, and I wondered what she saw when she did that, wondered what she was thinking, because I was thinking that I should get up and take a bath and go to her and hold her and let her cry and tell her that I loved her and that I would stop drinking and get a better job so that she could leave her job at the laboratory and go to medical school and become a doctor like she'd always dreamed of doing, and we would go to the park and have a meal in the sun and talk about nothing until the day was over, then lie down to sleep together and rise again in the morning and start over right there in the middle of summer, but I did not

VI

AND I ROW BACK TO SHORE IN THE AFTERNOON, A storm threatening in the west and the air becoming pungent with the electrical smell of ozone, the daylight turning green all of a sudden and giving the afternoon a feeling of everything happening as though on a stage, and it is this air and this light that remind me of coming home from work one day in late August of 1941 and Magda was gone with all her things, which weren't many, but they took up some space in our single chest of drawers and china cabinet for the china we would never have, the whole place quiet and thick and lonely-feeling, though the minute I opened the door I knew she was gone, and there was a letter on the kitchen table that said her mother wasn't well and she had taken the bus to Inkerman to be with her and she would come back—not come home, come back—when she could, and I waited for four months, until December of that year, when the country was finally at war, and even though I was married, I had no children and so received my Order to Report for Induction in the United States Army in late January, and on the day the letter stated I was to report I ate my breakfast of eggs and half a bottle of rye whiskey, packed clothes for three days, as the letter instructed, and trudged through snow down to the induction center and waited in a room full of men younger than I was until my name was called and they directed me to a curtained-off section, where a doctor in a white lab coat asked me to strip and looked at my naked body and thumped my back and put a stethoscope to my chest and stuck his fingers into my testicles and smelled my breath and asked me if I drank

Who doesn't, I said

and he made a note on his pad and I was told to go into another room, where there was another doctor, a tired-looking man in a lab coat whiter than the one the other physician wore, and the other physician handed this man the notes he had taken and I knew this was what they called the psychiatric evaluation, though he never told me he was a psychiatrist, he never told me anything, he sat down at a desk opposite the chair in which I was told to sit, studied what was written on the form, and then started asking me questions, the answers to which he knew from the form, like age, religion, schooling, parents living or deceased, and some that he did not

You're married, according to your form, he said

and I said yes and wondered out loud if this meant I wouldn't be drafted

It just lets me know you're not a homosexual, he said

and he asked me if there was any other reason why I would be unfit to serve in the United States Army

I've seen men die, I said

and he jotted that down

Where, he said

In a coal mine, I said

and he looked at me and I could see his eyebrows rise slightly, bushy ones like Štefan Bozak had, tiny gray wire brushes that graced the top of his face

Where, he said

The New Year's Mine Disaster, I said

and he wrote this down without looking up

I was the mule boy, I said

and he wrote this down too, and I told him again this was where I had seen men die and this was why I would not serve, would not fight, would not go to war, because I had seen death in men's faces, in their eyes by the light of nothing more than a carbide lamp shining from the peak of a cap, and I carried the faces of those men with me each day of my life, but I didn't tell him about the vow I'd made after I'd beaten bloody the schoolboy in Shenandoah who angered me with his filthy words about what happened in that mine, the real reason why I wouldn't serve, and then that psychiatrist wanted to know if I had committed any murders, if I was confessing to having murdered those men myself underground and that was what I was trying to tell the draft board by saying that I was refusing to serve because I had seen men die, and I said no, I was only a boy in the mines and those men looked out for me and I would be dead too if it hadn't been for them and a mule's rotting corpse, and he jotted this down on his pad of paper and asked again if I had ever killed anyone, if I had ever planned and carried out a murder, premeditated, he called it, and that lying about something like this would only add the crime of perjury to my sentence, and I began to feel trapped and claustrophobic, and I heard the voice of John Chibala say, You will live, Ondro, and I took a breath

I'm not a murderer, I said

and I breathed again

I don't believe in war, and I will not join an army or a navy, not even to serve in the ambulance corps, I said

and the psychiatrist wrote down one last note on my form and stood and handed the papers off to another man in a uniform, who read them and told me to move to another room, where I was told again I would be arrested and serve a prison term if I refused to be inducted into the United States Army, and I told him there is no such thing as prison, and he laughed and placed handcuffs around my wrists and I was held in a cell at the induction center alone that night, the guards refusing to speak to me or feed me, only giving me water and that just a cupful, like I was trapped in breast number seven again, until the morning, when they loaded me, still handcuffed, onto a bus with common criminals, boys who twitched and cocked their heads for toughness but who I could tell had been crying from the redness of their eyes, and men whose hands were cuffed like mine and whose eyes stared straight ahead, men who no doubt would have killed guard, driver, and anyone else who came close to them sure as those eyes could move, and we drove out of Wilkes-Barre north toward Scranton, where they separated me from the criminals and put me in a cell with urine-soaked drunks and bums arrested for petty theft, who derided me for being yellow-bellied and a coward when they found out I was in there because I had refused to be drafted, their words slurred with alcohol and derision, and it occurred to me that I hadn't had a drink in more than a day and I couldn't remember when that had been the case, except when Magda and I thought she might be pregnant, and I missed her, wished I could see her and talk to her, and I drank the water they gave me in a chipped and dirty porcelain cup, and I still had my three days' worth of clothes with me balled up in a paper bag, and my rosary in my pocket, but I wondered what would happen to the things I had left in my flat, I wondered what would happen to my Underwood typewriter and my Collected Shakespeare, if my landlord thought I had gone to war all of a sudden and had been killed and that was why I hadn't come back and so he might go ahead and try to sell my stuff, and then I wondered what he could get for a typewriter and an old book of plays, if anything, but that was all I had in the world now, those things and my rosary, and they meant something to me, and this is what I thought about as I sat there on the floor of that drunk tank shaking uncontrollably and vomiting piss-colored bile into my lap until all I could do was heave and heave and nothing came up anymore, sat there all day, until it occurred to me that Magda could get my stuff for me, if I wrote to her and asked her, and I decided that this was what I would do, and I fell asleep finally with my head against the wall and dreamed of nothing, not even wanting a drink, until the guard came in and kicked me in the side and told me to get up, they were taking me to Brooklyn, where I would serve out my prison sentence doing hard labor and thinking about my cowardice, and it was a deep, deep sleep from which I was emerging, so deep I feared again for a moment that my typewriter and my Shakespeare were gone forever, but then I remembered

I had decided to ask Magda to get them for me, and I shook off that sleep and felt the pain in my side and the rosary in my pocket and stood, and it was a four-hour trip to Brooklyn in the back of the prisoners' van, no food, no water, the van dark and empty of anything or anyone but me and the stench of me, and my body shook, and my mouth felt like someone had cleaned it out with a rag and left the rag in there and I would have killed for something to drink, but as the hours slipped by and the waning light outside made the van darker and darker inside, I knew where I was, and the peace and fear of being in the mines crept into that dark, the peace and fear I knew would accompany me all my life, prisoner to it no matter where, in the dark or light, though these many years later it does not hold me, does not frighten me, no matter where I lie down, and that first night in Brooklyn I lay in a small antechamber of a cell and listened to the traffic of the city outside and the rats scurrying along the floor in the dark inside, until morning, when guards came with keys and unlocked the cell and had me hand over my bag of clothes for three days and empty my pockets, and they took my rosary and told me to strip and hosed me down, then covered me in a powder that was meant to kill lice and gave me prison clothes and put me in the general population of murderers and thieves, and after a few days I stopped shaking and walked wherever they told me to walk when I was awake and slept in my cell at night like I hadn't slept since I was a boy, and it was in Brooklyn where I met Jacobson, a tall, handsome, and well-spoken man who could read and write in Greek, Latin, and Hebrew and talked of books and philosophers and quoted from Maimonides, Among them there is one to whom the lightning flashes only once in the whole of the night, and he had read the ancient pre-Socratic Parmenides in what fragmented Greek there remained of his writings, Jacobson having with him a manuscript he said he had borrowed permanently from Butler Library at Columbia University after they rejected his application a long time ago because of what he believed, borrowed permanently, he said, because they didn't deserve to have it, so few hands had touched it and would never read it, and it was Parmenides who, Jacobson said, understood the universe in all its singular mystery and fullness, and it was in the cafeteria among the general population my second week there, eating alone and looking scared, though I wasn't, when Jacobson sat down across from me and asked me not if but what and whom I had studied, and I said I had been a student of engineering for little more than a year, but I had read Shakespeare, and I told him about Professor Elias Gray and the day I asked him after class why we should read the man whose ideas of love and betrayal and heroics and death were entombed between the covers of books, and Professor Gray's eyes lit up and he told me that the Bard, as he called him, lived everywhere, asked me if I had ever been angry to the point of violence, and I said yes, and he asked me if I had ever sought to exact revenge, and I said yes, and he asked if I had ever felt that fear of betrayal that exists within the weakness of love, and I said yes, and he told me it was Shakespeare who knew of these more than anyone not because he had experienced them as a man, every man and woman knows these feelings well if they are alive for even one day, but because he knew the form of the drama, knew it as intimately as one knows a lover and wrote about the ways of all men and all women, wrote about them for the stage in the way that lovers accept and live by the strength and weakness of their love, because not to would be to accept a slow and agonizing death, as if by suffocation, and I nodded, knowing then why Professor Elias Gray read Shakespeare

You and I are going to be friends, Jacobson said

and I don't know why Jacobson was in prison in Brooklyn, what his crime was, but he told me I needed to declare myself a conscientious objector when I told him why I had been put there, it was a legal term and if I had a religious reason, or a moral reason, they legally had to honor that claim and not force me to fight, and they could only do certain things to me if the Selective Service approved it

As long as your lifestyle prior to claiming CO status reflects that claim, he said

and he sounded like he knew what he was talking about, and I asked him if he had claimed such a thing himself, and he said no, and looked away and ran his hand across his face from forehead to jaw like I used to do when I was between drinks and wondering where the next one was coming from

But I know the law and I can help you, he said

and Jacobson and I did become friends, he taught me how to protect myself in that place, how to keep from the mindless violence of the murderers and thieves, because serving our sentence didn't mean it was a just one, he used to say, only that it was our duty, and that too would make us strong, which I needed to hear because without him there I think I would have been devoured in that prison, in body and soul, but Jacobson told the other prisoners, who sought to devour bodies and souls almost impetuously, that I was mad, crazier than a chain gang in a lightning storm, because I had been trapped in a mine once, and I might even be a ghost of the man who actually died in that mine but who came back to haunt and torture criminal bastards like them, and if anyone so much as laid a hand on me, I would change, transform into something terrifying, something from the darkest depths of Hell, more terrifying than they had ever seen and would never want to see again, if they had eyes after that change and could see again, and they believed him and avoided me, avoided even being in the same corridor with me, and he told me to stare hard at them whenever we were in the general population and they would never touch me, and I did, and it gave me both a confidence and a sadness that those men were so childlike and lost that they could be deceived into living in fear like that, but it didn't mean they left Jacobson alone, or perhaps it was Jacobson who wouldn't leave them alone, he would come to lunch or dinner sometimes with his eye purpled or his jaw bruised so that he had to chew from the other side of his mouth, and when I asked him about it he would just say, A little resistance on the path of least resistance, or Water and necessary food, Ondro, water and necessary food, and in time, because we had plenty of time, Jacobson taught me how to play chess and how to read geometry from the volume of Euclid's Elements he had also smuggled into prison, and we began to read together, Plutarch and Parmenides and Herodotus the historian, and we read the translations Jacobson had been working on from the Greek, texts he had written down with a series of stubby pencils he was able to get from the guards whom he would help to finish high school or find their way into City College, even though they still treated him with contempt, but Parmenides was the philosopher Jacobson felt eluded him the most, an ancient who had much yet to teach the moderns, he said, teach them that their fear of death was weak and unfounded because there is no not being, and this is the only way we can live life and not fear death, knowing that to become nothing is impossible and that what matters is the being our bodies consist of and death is simply a change, Nor is there a way in which what-is could be / More here and less there, since all inviolably is, Jacobson often quoted from Parmenides, and he told me that we were in prison for our instruction and all we had done in life led us to this, and from here we would continue to take the path that was ours and ours alone, not because of anything destined or preordained but because there is no path other than the path we choose to take and death is not a destruction of being but a change of state, and it was on that day, when he spoke of Parmenides this way, that he seemed so noble to me I asked him why he was in prison, and he was quiet for a long time, then ran his hand from his forehead to his jaw

I angered the gods once by witnessing that change, when I was young and angry and resentful, he said

and he never spoke of why he was in prison again, and we had our hours of study and we had hours in which we talked when the forced labor they had given us to do in prison was over and in front of us was the labor of a kind of forced solitude, and one day Jacobson came into the library, where I was reading Pope's translation of the Iliad, and put some lined paper and one of his pencils in front of me

It's time you learned Hebrew, so you can read, he said

and I asked Jacobson what it was I could possibly read in Hebrew

The prophet Jonah, you'll see, not now, but you'll see, here is what I want you to practice, he said

and he had written out what he called the aleph bet and taught me how to follow from right to left, creating a kind of weaving back and forth of letters on those pages, front to back, then back to front and down each one until I had finished, after which I was to turn the pages over and do the same on the opposite side of the papers, a stack of about fifty pages, and I became fascinated with this and the letters and dots that made up the Hebrew aleph bet and practiced every day, creating my own stack of papers, and after almost six months of study in that prison I could write all of the Hebrew letters, and I showed Jacobson

Good, now we will read the prophet, every week we will read, on Friday, until you know, until you know, because there is lots of time in here and never enough, you'll see, he said and I thought of the way John Chibala used to talk in his stream of words carried along in his creek bed of thought and I missed him after all these years, and I missed Magda too, and after a time Jacobson noticed I received one and only one letter once a month, on or about the first of every month, and he asked me one day if there was anyone outside who knew I was here and was waiting for me, and I told him that, although I had been married, my wife and I had separated and she knew only that I had refused to be drafted and so was sent to prison, but she understood why, I didn't have to explain, even when I asked her in the first letter I wrote from prison if she would get my typewriter from the apartment before it was stolen, and she wrote back the next month saying she had driven to New York City with the typewriter and my Collected Shakespeare and left them in a pawnshop near the bus terminal in a neighborhood they called Hell's Kitchen, the claim ticket enclosed with the letter, and I told Jacobson that Magda was the only one who ever wrote to me, because there was no one else, my mother never wrote to me and I wondered at times if she was dead or alive, until I realized she didn't know I had gone to prison, unless Magda had told her, and time seemed to speed up and slow down with a consistent irregularity there in that prison, I read the ancients and studied Hebrew and began to read the prophet Jonah, and sometimes I found current fiction in the library, books that had been brought in by prisoners, or donated, or maybe even read and left by guards, I don't know, but I read Death Comes for the Archbishop, How Green Was My Valley, and For Whom the Bell Tolls, and I believed that perhaps I had begun to understand what the story of a fleeing man, in war and in peace, was all about, until on the first of the year in 1943 I received a letter that was dated December 24, 1942 and in which Magda wrote to ask for an annulment of our marriage because a priest had told her that, given the circumstances of my life and the fact that we had no children together, it spoke of God's will, and she had come to believe too that it was God's will for us not to be together under the bond of holy matrimony, but most of all because she had found someone who did not carry what I carried, and he wanted to marry her, though she would not until our marriage was annulled, and would I grant that request so that she could be married again to a man who would take care of her, A man, she wrote, who saw light when he looked into my eyes, and would I do that for her, if I loved her, not in body but in spirit and soul, and I wrote back to her and said yes, I understood, though it was not true that I saw no light when I looked into her eyes, I saw a darkness, yes, but I saw there too what I hoped for in life, a hope placed in me by the man who had given her life, and a few weeks later I received a letter from the Diocese of Scranton with papers in it, papers I was meant to sign to begin the process of marriage annulment, and I placed the letter and those papers under my cot and thought nothing more of them, until the day a prison chaplain came to my cell, a man who did not look as though he had ever spent any time in a prison, as chaplain or otherwise, and he asked me if we could speak, though there were bars between us, and I said yes, and he asked if I was Ondro Prach, if I was married to Magda Chibala Prach, and if I had chosen to go to prison rather than go to war in the service of my country, and I said yes to all three questions, and he asked me if I wanted to confess anything, and he carried a stole with him, one I remember the priest from the mining patch wore in the confessional when I went to confession as a boy and confessed to him things a boy confesses, like having yelled Dammit! when I pinched my finger as a nipper, and wondering if there really was a God when I sat in the darkness of the mine, to which he, the priest from the patch, smiling behind the screen, would say, Oh Ondro, ňestaraj śe, God is alive, now try not to take his name in vain, and he would give me two Pater Nosters and an Ave Maria to say for my penance, but the chaplain in prison asked me if I wanted to make my confession for sins I had committed, because he had seen my papers and sometimes men do things they don't understand but still need to confess before God for the salvation of their souls and the souls of the men they watched die, and I looked at him as he placed his stole around his shoulders, a man not much older than I was at the time, his eyes and face and weak frame bearing something of a man who has never had to fight, never wanted to fight, in body or soul, his choice one of accepting all that has been laid upon him, and I said nothing, and he turned his head sideways with his ear to my face, not as though to hear me better but as though we were in complete darkness and only sound could pass between us, and still I said nothing

You don't have anything to confess, he said

and I am sure he meant it as a question, but I looked at the side of his head because we weren't in complete darkness, we were on two sides of bars in a cell and the uncovered lightbulb above us gave off its harsh and unforgiving light and he remained with his head turned to the side, his ear waiting to hear the confession he was certain I would give, but I said nothing and stared at his slumped shoulders, at his bloodless and clean-shaven face, and he seemed to sense my gaze and leaned away from the bars in that light and turned his head slightly toward me as if to steal a glance, as if he feared I might pass through those bars, and I don't know what he saw in my eyes but I saw nothing in his, and he made the sign of the cross, not to bestow a blessing upon me but to protect himself in the way superstitious believers will make the sign of the cross for protection

And the men feared greatly and they said to him, What is this you have done, I said

and I recited these words in Hebrew, words the priest did not know, and he stood quickly and removed the stole from his shoulders and walked from the room and I walked over to the cot in my cell, reached beneath it for the papers I had put there weeks ago, filled them out and gave them to the guard in charge of the mail, and by the autumn of that year Magda and I were no longer husband and wife, and Jacobson and I sat out of the rain in the yard on a cold day in October and did not play chess or discuss philosophy or read Shakespeare to each other from a copy of Hamlet he had found in the library, he did something he never did as we sat and listened to the rain falling through a downspout and dripping from the roof, he asked me which of the miners died with the most dignity, which one did I think had the happiest death, and I wasn't ready for that question, I wasn't ready to do anything but serve the rest of my time as a conscientious objector and wait for the war to be over, because I hadn't met yet, or told anything to, any of the children or the grandchildren of the miners and their butties, except Magda Chibala, and even she never asked me about her father's final days and hours underground, but I think Jacobson saw the change in me over the years that came with the reading and the conversation and the time I had to think about what I had done, and what I had failed to do, my mind clear of the alcohol, my heart clear of the sadness and guilt that I had been neither a good husband to the only woman I had ever loved nor father to the family I would never have, and I sat on that slab of concrete out of the rain like a nipper at the opening of a ventilation door, the car coming and the light from the headlamp of the spragger with it, and I thought about how, in those first two days, the butties had died, the butty Emil crushed and the butty Matty bleeding to death from his severed hand, thought about it not with the detail I would use years later to tell the children and grandchildren and great-grandchildren of those butties, because I hadn't had the time, and I needed the time, but with enough clarity of mind to think about what it meant to find in those mines a happy death, and I told Jacobson that once we knew where we were in that mine, John Chibala and Štefan Bozak and I, and knew we weren't going to suffocate from black damp, the three of us tried to figure how we were going to get ourselves out of what was left of breast number seven, and so we talked about a plan, or rather, John Chibala and Štefan Bozak talked and I listened, the two of them nearly breathless themselves from their own injuries, Štefan slowly going into shock, I know now, but focused on finding a way out of that room in the same way he had focused on robbing the pillars of the breast, and they talked in the dark and I worked by the light, picking up rocks where the collapse had been at the entrance and rolling them away because they were big and I was a boy then, but there was only so much room in there and any rocks I pulled away had to be moved to where there was room, and Štefan Bozak could move, though erratically when he did, but John Chibala sat on the floor with broken legs and a broken back and couldn't move, and Jacobson stared ahead as I told him this, not in disbelief but as though he understood, as though he had once looked upon this same scene

This is how men look when they are looking at death, he said

and I was caught by his stare until I remembered his question again, and I told Jacobson it was the miner Štefan Bozak who never gave up, who gave me his carbide and told me where to dig, who determined how long we would keep the lamp lit and how much rock I ought to move in the light of that lamp, his voice ragged and breathy as he directed me and encouraged me, even when a rock rolled from the pile and onto my foot and out of fear that I'd be crushed or crippled I sat in the shadowy light of the lamp and began to cry, and Štefan Bozak put his hand on my shoulder

We're going to be fine, Ondro, ňestaraj śe, he said

and he told me we had to get enough of the collapse pile pulled away to open an access point, even if just to use our voices to let them know we were in there and that we were alive, and he would wheeze when he took a breath, and I could see him wince when I turned to be sure it was he who was actually speaking to me, and then we snuffed the light and passed around the growler with the beer in it, which wasn't much because they had all shared it during lunch, and we had given some to Matty before he died, but Štefan Bozak told me not to let even a little go to waste

We'll rest for a while and fire the lamp and start again in an hour, he said

and then, for a moment, I couldn't go on, and I told Jacobson I had never told anyone that much about my time underground with those men, it was years before the others would come to me, and the memory of John Chibala and Štefan Bozak in those days and hours before their deaths brought me to tears, the only time in prison I ever cried, and I missed Magda and wished I had told her before we were married what I was telling Jacobson about her father and her father's friend, and I could not take in air all of a sudden and Jacobson pulled himself out of his stare and put his hand on my shoulder and told me to breathe, and my breath stuttered as I inhaled and tried to keep back the tears of that grief, and Jacobson said I could try another day, we had a long time left to our sentences yet

No, I want to tell this, I want to tell you this, I want you to know too if there was any dignity in these deaths, I said

and he nodded and took his hand from my shoulder and turned his body on the cement slab on which we sat so that he could look straight at me instead of into the yard, and I told him that when Štefan Bozak gave me that taste of beer I felt it go straight to my head and thought I would sleep there and wake up and it would be morning again, someplace where there was morning, and I put my head against the damp wall but I couldn't sleep for Štefan Bozak's wheezing, and he seemed to know and shifted and groaned

I'm worried about Johnny, he said

and I didn't say anything

Ondro, we need to get you out of here so that you can get some help for Johnny, he said

But Matty and Emil, I said

They are with God now, ňestaraj śe, but it's not your time, you're in here to work, he said

and I had never spoken with Štefan Bozak the miner before, he wasn't family and boys in the mines didn't speak to miners, but he was kinder than any man I knew, he and John Chibala, and I felt a closeness to him then, felt the closeness of death, I know now, but also the longing I think I have always felt for my father, and I listened to him wheeze in the darkness and the damp, knowing that we would all be with God soon

How do we know when it's our time, I said

and Štefan Bozak gave a small laugh

You didn't wake up today expecting this, he said

No, I said

No, but here we are awake and talking like any other day, and like no other day you'll ever have for the rest of your long life, he said

How do you know, how do you know I'll have a long life, I said

I don't, I believe, and that's enough, he said

and he coughed and groaned

Listen to me, it hit me pretty hard in the ribs and side, that damn rock, I can't get a breath, he said

and he tried to turn his body in the dark, as though the rock rested on him still, but there was no rock and little room and he groaned again

Yes, I have to believe, he said

and he was quiet for a while, taking short and shallow breaths, so that I thought he had gone to sleep, until he spoke with a peace that had seemed to come over him

I just wish I could see them again, mojo dzeci, one more time asleep in their beds, he said

and he meant his children, his six children, not one of them older than twelve in that year, on that day

I keep them in mind when I work, not in the front of my mind, because there's work to do and I keep my work in the front of my mind, but in the back of it, always in the back, where they're safe, mojo dzeci, safe at home asleep in their beds, where I left them, he said

and he took a breath, or tried to take a breath, a deep breath, but he could not, and he tried again, gasped, and gave that whimper and breathed slow and shallow breaths until he seemed to get enough to speak

Because it's why I do this, why I kiss them all on the forehead in the morning before the sun and kiss my Jana and walk from that patch to the lift, and I keep them with me all day long, even now, and they will be there with me whether or not I come out of this ground, he said

and he inhaled a few more ragged breaths and I could feel his chest rise and fall in the dark, he was so close to me, and I wanted to say, How do you know, because we weren't safe there underground, and although I didn't know how to think of it then, Štefan must have known this would be his last day of work underground, must have known this when he said good-bye to the children he left sleeping that morning and wanted every morning only to keep safe

Drink some water, Mr. Bozak, I said

and I could hear him shake his head, hear the collar of his jacket ruffle and the lamp on his cap move a bit and he took another small breath and whimpered

My Jana will kiss them in the morning each day and tell them how much I loved them and how I used to bounce them on my knee, each one of them, he said

and his breaths were getting shorter now, as though he were sipping at the water he had just refused to drink

She'll remind them of how I taught my oldest to swim at the quarry, and taught my daughter Rose to whittle with a knife, and how I sang to the others, each one of them, and how I loved to give them all a taste of beer when I opened a bottle, he said

and I lit the carbide because I was afraid, and I could see him smiling in the light, the smile I remember when I think of the name Štefan Bozak

Yes, Jana will tell them and they will grow up knowing their father loved them, and they will grow to be fathers and mothers themselves, with the help of God, he said

and he coughed hard and cried out in pain, or

what must have been pain, because I heard him whimper once more, though from the pain or the thoughts of his children I couldn't say, but he did and there was quiet for a long time in the dark, although his cry had woken John Chibala, who groaned and shifted from where he sat on the floor

Ondro, he said

and he sounded out of breath, or in his own pain, and he grimaced and clenched his teeth as he moved, his eyes closed, not knowing I was watching him, until he took what deep breath he could and let it out and opened his eyes again

Ondro, you've lit the lamp, let's see if we can move more of that rock, let Štefan sleep, he said

and Jacobson kept watching me all this time, watching and listening, as though I were elsewhere, he said to me later, waiting for me to finish, but he was listening and nodding, then spoke from the prophet Jonah, You turn us back to dust, and say, Turn back, and then we listened to the water in the downspout drip intermittently now that the rain in the prison yard was over

This is the memento mori, my friend, the reminder of death, these men lived with it and understood it better than any ancient, Jacobson said

They only wanted to get out, I said

They wanted you to get out, he said

and I looked around at where I was, a prison no better than the mine in which those men died, and

I wondered if Jacobson feared I might not come back from that descent down into the mine this time, because he spoke with a voice that a father might use to comfort a child

Tell me what happened next, he said

and so I took a breath and paused as I listened to the dripping water and told him that after John Chibala had given me those instructions, I turned around and, in the light of the carbide, could see Štefan Bozak with his head slumped onto his chest like a man sleeping and I thought for a moment that he was dead, but I could see his chest rising and falling, not with deep breaths but with breaths nevertheless, and I turned to look at the pile of rock that had sealed us in, looked to see if there was any way I could find to get us out

Pull at those smaller pieces of slag at the top and let Štefan sleep, John Chibala said

and I pulled at the sharp and broken pieces of shale and rock that lay at the top of the pile, a pile reaching to the ceiling, and it began to crumble and slide and I had to back away fast, but that opened a small break in the mass of rock at the top and I climbed up and reached my hand in, and behind the scree was stone that stood like a wall in front of whatever was on the other side

You're through, can you see into the chamber, John Chibala said

It's all rock, I said

and he was quiet for a moment, breathing, but breathing hard, I could hear him

It's resting on another slab underneath, if you find that point there will be a gap, a crack, some fissure you can crawl through, there will be, he said

and he spoke these words with the matter-of-factness of a man who knows his work, a man who can see it in front of him, can lay his hands to it even when it is no more than the idea of work in his mind, and I pulled at the scree and rock with a nervousness that came from my desire to get out of there, to be out in the open again, and I felt my hand slice on a piece of sharp slate, and I hollered, Dammit! in the small room

Don't, Ondro, you'll only get hurt, save the light and let's think about where you should dig next, John Chibala said

and I extinguished the carbide on the hat I wore, the hat that was Štefan Bozak's, and I sat in the dark facing John Chibala and listened to him breathe

Grab that growler collecting groundwater and take a drink, then pass it to me, I'm thirsty, he said

and I knew where the growler was in that small room of pitch-black, the plinking drip of water from the ceiling still making an intermittent splash into what had become a few inches of water, and I reached for it there in the dark and put the brim of it to my lips and took a sip, the drink tasting cold and a little like sulfur, but it quenched my thirst and made me wonder if I would ever taste water again after that, and I handed the growler to John Chibala and heard him take a long drink from the bucket, then almost gasp, and he handed it back to me

Štefan will need a drink when he wakes up, he said

and I put the growler on the floor beneath the drip from the ceiling and it made a plinking sound again as the water hit the steel bottom, once, twice, a few more times, and then settled into a quiet splash, and I felt angry, angry that I was as unable to move in that room as these men who were pinned beneath and wounded by rock

Will they find us, Mr. Chibala, I said

I don't know, Ondro, I'd rather take my chances with you getting out and finding them, he said

But the rock, I said

Is all around us and we have to find a way through, it's too bad we can't get to that dynamite box, but that would be dangerous in here, he said

and he said this in a rush, as though he were thinking out loud and gave a quick laugh at the idea that we might use dynamite now to get ourselves out, and I thought to tell him that there was no dynamite in the box, but it didn't matter anymore

Wake up Štefan and ask him if he thinks there ought to be a fissure in that rock, he said and I turned toward Štefan Bozak and moved the few feet there were between us on the floor

Mr. Bozak, I said

and I touched him on the shoulder and gave him a little shake, but he didn't move, didn't even cry out, and I didn't feel the breath from him that I could see before in the light, but I shook him again and still there was no sound, no movement, no waking anymore

Oh Štefan, they're going to miss us, I know, but God will provide for every last one, ňestaraj śe, John Chibala said

VII

AND IT MIGHT YET RAIN TODAY, THE CLOUDS ARE building in the west that way, but it's hard to say, so I leave the windows of the house open and pour a glass of iced tea and walk out to the porch built in the shadow of the big white pine and I sit down and stare at the mountain, its green face and ridgeline deeper-looking in this light of late summer, and I take up the prophet Jonah again but I don't read because sometimes I remember Jacobson in ways that keep me from being able to do anything, like the way in which a turn of phrase reminds me of him, or the way in which I will see someone from behind and think just for a moment that it is he and perhaps fate has put us on the same path again, even if that's no longer possible, and I think it's because today is a Friday, just as it was on the day in December when Jacobson came to sit with me at dinner, and I had been given a letter by a guard that had come the day before, a letter from the United States Forest Service, asking me if I would be willing to do my part in wartime conservation and serve as a fire lookout in the mountains and forests of New England in lieu of serving a prison term, and after I had read the letter myself I gave it to Jacobson and he read it and put it down and seemed to smile to himself

You convinced them, he said

and I didn't know what he meant and said that there wasn't anyone I needed to convince of anything

Well, I convinced them, I wrote a letter requesting conscience objector status, told them about my moral objection to war, the why, where, and how of it, and signed your name, he said

and he said I should consider the offer seriously because he saw prison was weakening me and no one knew how long the war would go on, and so I wrote back and told them I would accept their offer if it meant I would no longer have to serve the length of my prison term, and after months of waiting, I received a letter in April saying my release date was the twenty-ninth of April and there would be a work truck waiting to pick me up at the train station in Jaffrey, New Hampshire, on the first of May, and the day before my release I was with Jacobson in the prison yard and he handed me a brown envelope with papers inside

So that you don't forget what I taught you, so that you'll stop running from what it is you're running from and find your place beneath some tree, he said

and he spoke again in the same way John

Chibala spoke, like the way creek water moves, and I took the papers out and, written in pencil on the title page, one of the many pencils I knew he kept hidden in his cell and sharpened against the rough concrete wall until they were no more than a nub, was the Hebrew word יוֹנָה and on eight pages of paper written large enough for me to read was the Hebrew text of the book of Jonah written in Jacobson's blocky script, and I flipped through it back to front and could understand every word he had written, not just because I had studied the book to the point of having memorized it but because he had taken such care to make the script beautiful in his own hand, and I thanked him, and early the next day the guard on duty gave me the bag with three days of clothes in it that I had taken to the induction center, the letter Magda Chibala had written to me about my typewriter, the claim ticket for the pawnshop, and the rosary I always kept in the pocket of my trousers but had to surrender the first night I arrived in Brooklyn, and the guard handed all of these to me as if they were a few coins, or a set of keys, or anything else a man might have had in his pockets on the day he went to prison, and I took the rosary last, and when I touched it, touched the small carved cross attached to the string of horsehair lined with oblong beads spaced in decades in a circle, I touched my father, and my mother, and Magda, who had for a moment in the hot sun out at the lake on the day we were married let the wood of those beads receive her, and I was thrown back into a world in which nothing and everything had changed, and I wanted to kneel and weep and say an Ave Maria, but the guard was watching and he had only my discharge on his mind that day

Let's go, Prach, put all that stuff away so we can get you out of here, he said

and I changed into the clothes I hadn't worn in almost three years, a little baggy on me now, and put my rosary and Magda's letter and the claim ticket for the pawnshop in my pocket, and kept the rest of my clothes in the bag with the Hebrew text of the prophet Jonah, and I walked to the guardhouse at the entrance of the prison and looked back to see if Jacobson had somehow managed to convince a guard to let him come this far to see me off, but he wasn't there, and both guards at the door said good-bye, as though I were one of them, and the one who had been there the longest thanked me for not causing any trouble, and I lifted my hand as if to say good-bye, or that I never wanted any trouble, then lowered my hand and my head and walked out into Brooklyn and took the bus from the Navy Yard into Manhattan and got off at the Port Authority and sat on a bench in the terminal, which smelled of cigarette smoke and cleaning fluid, and I opened the envelope with Magda's letter in it and the claim ticket for the pawnshop with the address Forty-first

Street and Eleventh Avenue written on it, and I stood up and walked outside and down a block and west to Eleventh Avenue, where I found the pawnshop and went inside and gave an old Irishman the claim ticket, and he looked it over and laughed like I hadn't heard a man laugh since I was a boy and handed the ticket back to me

Sold that years ago, he said

But she told you to hold on to it, I said

and he raised his arm slowly and pointed to the sign on the door

It says Pawnshop, not Storage Locker, lad, he said

and he laughed again and raised his eyebrows

Pretty girl, she was, but a damn sight dour man what brought her, he said

and the smile left him

What about my Shakespeare, I said

and all in one move he scowled, shook his head, and cursed under his breath, then turned and walked into a room in the back that looked like a storage room to me and came out and threw my Collected Shakespeare on the counter

There, Shakespeare, the one your girlfriend gave me to hold on to because I'm the fucking New York Public Library, now get the fuck out of here before I change my mind, professor, he said

and I walked back to the bus station with my book in one hand and my bag in the other and my rosary in my pocket and waited for the bus to Boston and got on, and it was night when we arrived and I walked to the railroad station, the cool ocean air along the Boston waterfront smelling of brine and coal smoke, and I slept in the station and caught the morning train for Brattleboro and got off in Winchendon, Massachusetts on the first of May and took another train into Jaffrey, New Hampshire, where the work truck was waiting for me, just as the letter said, and the truck drove me to the guard station at the base of Mount Monadnock, where I was assigned to an old fire tower, a groundhouse built near the treeless summit, which didn't sit much more than three thousand feet above sea level, and I did the rest of my sentence as a conscientious objector alone there on the mountain, except when hikers came by to see what it was they had discovered tucked into a notch of two massive rounds of granite with seams of crystal running through them from another time, when the rock emerged from that ground in molten blasts hot enough to fuse those seams inside it, that's where they found me, sunburned and filthy and looking out over the Worcester Plateau in search of fire in Massachusetts to the south, New Hampshire to the north and east, and Vermont to the west, a draft-dodging hermit who had refused to go to war and was protected by the United States Forest Service, so indifferent to the arrival and requests of its personnel that they thought me deaf or dangerous and departed, but I was up with the sun every morning that summer, long before the hikers, and I searched the vernal pools at the summit for signs of life and found frogs and salamanders and water skimmers and sometimes a box turtle that had wandered too far above the trail, and I watched herds of deer and once quietly avoided a bear that was no doubt already avoiding me and never saw so much as a scat sign of the puma the locals all said still lived up there, as though they would welcome that companion along the trail, though I would be happy not to, and when I wasn't hiking around the old and rugged mountain I sat in the groundhouse and read Shakespeare until the daylight waned and I tucked into my sleeping bag and slept until the sun rose in the east over Thorndike Pond and woke me again, and in the fall when the rains came and winter was imminent, I came down off the mountain and rented a small room in the Ark Hotel, which catered to prominent guests in the summer but took my money and charged me less for the same room in the winter, and winter in New Hampshire was so long and cold and punishing I wondered at times if the earth and all around would ever be warm again, but spring somehow always came, and then the summer, and I went back to my lookout on Monadnock and watched for fire and hiked and read Shakespeare and the prophet Jonah in Hebrew every Friday for another year, and when the war was over I received a letter from the government saying that my prison sentence was also over and I was being released from my duties with the United States Forest Service and could choose to apply for peacetime employment with the New Hampshire Forestry and Recreation Commission because I was not a felon, and so I did and they hired me to man a guard station at the entrance to Monadnock State Park in the summer, and I stayed in Jaffrey through September of 1946 and in October found a house to live in on Thorndike Pond in exchange for caretaking, and I took another job at a boarding school down the road in Dublin, splitting firewood and delivering it to the houses and dormitories of faculty and students, and though I found no one there who would speak to me of Hebrew Scripture, as Jacobson had, or Shakespeare, as Professor Elias Gray had, I did find a book on a table in one of the dormitory common rooms, next to the fireplace, Early Greek Philosophy, by John Burnet, inside of which was a chapter on Parmenides of Elea and a translation of the fragments, and so I tucked it into my winter coat with a peaceful sense of impunity and kept that book for myself and read the chapter on Parmenides over and over in the evenings, and I missed Jacobson and wondered where he had gone and what he was doing now that the war was over, though I knew where he was and what his days would be like for the rest of his life, war or no war, but I still wanted to talk to him about what message from God he and I both, it seemed, were running from, if there was a God in the end, a God we loved, hidden and standing right before us, standing the distance of a breath away, With the help of God, as Štefan Bozak used to say, until the moment of our deaths, be they shameful or dignified, in pain or at peace, or if all were simply a matter of letting one life change for another, because there is no not being, It is all one to me where I begin, for I shall come back again there, and I find myself whispering that line still throughout the day, every day, sometimes after I have finished my reading of the prophet Jonah in Hebrew, sometimes the last thing I remember to speak before I blow out the lamp and go to sleep, and after the man whose house I rented on Thorndike Pond passed away, I purchased it and made it my own, building furniture with wood from the land that surrounds it and bookshelves I filled with books I found all over the state, collections of literature and poetry, books on engineering and science and architecture, and even a section dedicated to the history of coal mining and famous mine disasters, not one of which mentions the New Year's Mine Disaster, and I have lived a long time alone here on the pond, throughout all the years I worked at the ranger station on the mountain and came home to my rough-hewn furniture and my collection of books and the cries of the loons rising up from the water, the only cries I hear from anything that sounds ghostlike anymore, to my last day of work there, the day I told the son and grandson and great-grandson of the butty Emil Milenec about how the man died and what words were on his lips, and the same day, a Friday in summer two years later, when I told the daughter and the granddaughter of the butty Matty Holub about how the man died and what words were on his lips, and all of them went back to their homes in Pennsylvania and went to sleep knowing what was in those men's hearts when they died so long ago, what they had done, what they had failed to do, but there is still one person who has yet to come, and though I don't believe she ever will, I still wait for her and think of her often, not every day, but on those days she comes to mind in the way a hawk will block the sun for a moment when it's flying close to the ground, the opposite of a flash of light, the flash of shadow, that is how I think of Magda Chibala, wondering where she lives, if she is happy with the husband who loves her in the way I could not have loved her, if she has children, a son perhaps, with the teeth and grin of his grandfather, but I only wonder about her in those moments I have in between the work I do to maintain order in my world here, it is what I learned and have carried with me from the mines, so I cut back the high grass in the meadow, take down the birch that split during an ice storm in the winter, rebuild the sagging wall that shapes the bed of flowers along the front of the house, and pull weeds from those beds and between the stone steps that lead down the path to the pond, and then I have to rest, and it is when I am rowing to shore in my boat, or reading in the chair I made from a red oak the sawyer took from the woods by the house and had milled for me, as I am now, that I think of Magda, let myself think of Magda, and when I look up today I see the clouds that once were threatening a summer storm have begun to disperse and there will be no rain, I can tell, the afternoon has reached that hour for which no one has ever come up with a name, as far as I know, the sun going down but not quite set, the air cooler for the lateness of the day this late in the season, not as heavy and humid as it was when the storm threatened hours ago, so windless the birds stopped singing and the mosquitoes came in waves, but a breeze has picked up with a freshness to it and I put my pages of Jonah into the wooden box I made for them and go inside and place it on the bookshelf next to my Collected Shakespeare, but instead of going back out onto the porch to sit beneath the white pine, something is drawing me to the pond, the loons perhaps, or maybe because I know the change in air pressure will mean the perch should start to bite and I would like some fresh fish for dinner, and so I walk out the back door and down to the pond, where two loons are swimming offshore and hooting at each other, neither one far from its mate, their bodies black-and-white-feathered, low in the water and looking strangely ancient, as though they have risen up from the depths of the pond from some prehistoric sleep, and I take my bait bucket from the boat and start turning over rocks at the water's edge and in a few minutes I have three crayfish and think I may be lucky this afternoon, because the air is fresh and the water is cool, and I check my fishing gear and walk out along the shore to a point of land where the water moves a little faster because the far shore is closer here, and I cast my baited hook out into the cut, let it drift, reel it in and cast again, and in an hour I have two good-sized perch, one I'll eat for my dinner tonight and one I'll save for tomorrow, and the loons are still hooting because they are never far from each other, they only wail when they're apart, and I take my creel of fish and walk up the path to the house and into the kitchen, and I know there is someone here, someone here in the house with me, it's the air, it has been moved through and not by me, and I'm afraid at first because no one ever comes to this house without my seeing them before they see me, but in the wake of that movement there is a familiarity, a recognition, a memory of a time all its own, a time when all I knew was darkness and fear, and I know who it is and where she is, and why, and I put the fish in the sink and walk out to the porch and Magda Chibala is sitting in my chair beneath the white pine, the one in which I was reading the prophet Jonah two hours ago, and she turns and looks at me as I emerge from the house and step out onto the boards of the porch, as though I were the visitor and she has lived here all these years, and still, even after I have felt her presence and have seen her in the chair, I think for a moment she may yet be a flash of shadow, so I look up at the top of the mountain as if to clear my sight and back at the chair beneath the tree and she is still there, and I walk toward her and sit down in the chair next to her, the chair in which the son of Emil Milenec sat, and she looks up at the mountain too, the sun beginning to set behind it, then back at me

I've been waiting for you, she says

and her hair is still long and black, though she has tied it in a ponytail behind her back and a few strands of gray lay in wisps across her forehead, not wild like when she was a girl but untamed in what way they can be above the eyes that match them now gray for gray, and she is wearing a light dress for the August heat and lace-up boots that look as though she has gone farther than down the road in them, and a leather suitcase with a CPO jacket like a man would wear are on the porch boards next to her

I was fishing, I say

and she nods and looks up at the mountain again, as if she can't decide which old face she wants to study, and I think she still might be some kind of revenant and will leave like all the others, and so I close my eyes when I see her look up again and open them before she has turned back, so that, if she catches me, it might look only as though I want to sleep

I see why you never left here, never came back to Pennsylvania, even for a visit, she says

and a late-day cicada buzzes, and a woodpecker knocks away at the pine

That's what the others said to me too, I say

and we sit in our silence and let the chorus of birds and breeze and insects make up the symphony of a late-August afternoon in New Hampshire

Would you like to stay for dinner, I have fresh fish, I say

Yes, thank you, she says

I'll make tea first, I say

Tea would be nice, she says

and I make the tea the ranger still brings me from the store in Harrisville, and when we are done with tea I gut the fish and cut some onions and the carrots I picked, and I pan-fry the fish and onions and boil the carrots, and all we talk about is the tea and the food and the weather and my house, and the nights have begun to cool considerably at the end of summer, so after dinner I lay a fire in the fireplace and we sit before it and I ask her if she is tired from her travels and if she would like to sleep and have a breakfast of blueberries and coffee in the morning, but she just stares into the fire and doesn't speak

Magda, I say

Sleep can wait, she says

and I know her, I know the girl who would stand outside of church to see me and outside the store to ask where I've been, or write to me to say, Come visit, or wait at my side while I dropped further and further down into darkness, yes, she would have waited seemingly forever, until she couldn't wait any longer, and I think to myself that I don't want to sleep either, not with her here by my side again, but I know that the sleep she abjures tonight must be because there is a story I do not know about her, and so this time I will wait for her, wait for her to begin to speak, and she does, in time, there before the fire I have laid in my house in the mountains, slowly and in a roundabout manner she speaks about the intervening years, telling me her mother had passed away not long after I had written to Magda from prison about my typewriter and after she had written to me asking for the annulment, and yet how all of that seems so long, long ago

We're orphans now, I say

We're all orphans, she says

and we sit and listen to the fire burn with the

deep hum and intermittent snap with which a good fire burns

And you're traveling with the man's jacket but not the man, I say

It's safer that way, she says

and after yet another long silence, she tells me that she met the man in the hospital where she worked in the lab, he ran the cafeteria and the food services and they struck up a conversation when he sat with her at lunch one day, asked her where she was from and she told him it was a place known only for one day, a day that had shaped her entire life, and he said that he had heard of the mine and was sorry for the men who had died down there, and when he asked if she was alone she told him her husband was in prison because he had avoided the draft, and he said he understood why some men couldn't serve but not why others wouldn't and spoke about how he couldn't serve because he wanted to enlist in the navy but had a heart murmur and here he was, feeding a hospital, and they began to have lunch together every day, and then they went to see a movie together at the Forty Fort Theater, and she felt she had betrayed me for this, but it also seemed to her as though I was always in a prison and, it hurt her to say, it became clear to her that our marriage could never last, no matter how badly one or both of us wanted it to, and in a short amount of time the man began to change from a friend she had lunch with to someone who was instructing her on how she could get an annulment in the case of our marriage, and when Magda Chibala asked him why she should do this, he told her that he too dreamed of being happily married and having children and filling an entire pew with his family in church

Everything he said was true, about his family, about the annulment, about going to Mass, and you began to fade from me until I believed you would remain in your prison forever, she says

and after I had signed the papers and the annulment came through, they got engaged and visited her mother and aunt in Inkerman and she thought nothing of it at the time, but she remembers he was strangely familiar, solicitous almost, with the aunt who was taking care of her mother, but that summer Magda Chibala and the man she would not name were married

And on our wedding night he got sick and I cared for him until he got better and we went up to the Poconos for a weekend as a kind of honeymoon, but he was ill up there as well, I don't know what it was, Ondro, he was good to me at first, endearing you might call it, even going so far as to accompany me to New York to put your typewriter in hock at that pawnshop near the bus station, but we were never intimate with each other, she says

and I realize she speaks in the same way her father used to speak Slovak, and I let her speak, not telling her what happened to the typewriter because, after all these years here in my house on the pond in the shadow of a mountain, the typewriter means no more to me than being an orphan means anything to an old man, and she thinks my distraction means I don't want to hear about this man to whom she was married, but I tell her I do, if she has to tell me about him, and she nods

Yes, I do, she says

and so she asked him one day if there was something wrong, if she didn't please him, if he found her unattractive, and he told her he loved her and it was only a matter of time before they would start having children, he wanted to make sure his job was secure and he wanted to move out of the apartment they were renting on the east side of Wilkes-Barre and into a house, and she told him that didn't mean they couldn't share the same bed and the intimacies of that bed, but still he did nothing, and it got so that he would not even touch her, and one day she went to Inkerman alone to see her mother and found out from the aunt that her husband had been coming around asking about Mrs. Chibala and telling the aunt that, as the man of the family now, he had a right to know the details of her property and finances, and the aunt made a sweeping gesture with her hand to encompass the old house on the side of the road that ran past culm bank after culm bank, and a month later her mother died and the man had in fact looked into the woman's estate and assets and found out she had received the largest settlement of all the miners from the New Year's Mine Disaster, a payout of ten thousand dollars, which had been sitting in bonds and certificates of deposits since Magda was a girl, and the amount was now close to one hundred thousand dollars, and the man took it all, but Magda had already suspected there was something like this going on when, one night after dinner, one week after her mother had died, she asked him again why it was they never shared a bed, and he changed then, as if in a moment, and told her they hadn't shared a bed because he'd never wanted children with her and never would, and when, as if bewildered, she asked why, he told her he had now what he wanted and she wondered what he wanted

Because all I've ever wanted was to love and be loved, she says

and I look down because I have known this more than I have known anything in my life, and she tells me that, one night after dinner, his ambitions still a mystery to her, she rose to carry to the sink the dishes from that dinner and he put his foot out and tripped her and she stumbled and dropped the dishes and they crashed to the floor and shattered, and he laughed and called her a clumsy bitch, and when she knelt down to pick up the broken pieces he kicked her hard in the stomach and growled, I'm not putting anything in there, and the next day she packed a bag with the things of hers she wanted and left the old flat on the east side of Wilkes-Barre and took a bus up the line to Inkerman and knocked on the door of the house where her mother had lived and where she knew her aunt was still living, and her aunt answered and looked at her on the porch of the house and shook her head and said, Now I have nothing because of you, and she closed the door in Magda's face, and Magda sits in the chair by the fire in my house and the fire cracks because I have just put a birch log on, and, though it is cool outside, I have left the windows open and the sound of the loons is a wail now, one searching for the other in the darkness, and she tells me that after she left her aunt, she took the bus into Wilkes-Barre again and at the station got a bus down the line for Shenandoah and knocked on the door of my mother's house

She thought you were the reason I dropped out of college, the reason I did everything I did, and she wasn't wrong, I say

You never wrote to her from prison, she says

I never wanted to, I say

But she wanted you to, she says

I don't know that that's true, I say

It's true, she says

and now I stare into the fire and we are silent and the loons continue to wail in their search for each other

But she didn't know where you were, it was as if you had disappeared, she says

I did, I say

and Magda says nothing more and the fire cracks and the wail of the loons rises up from the pond and into the open window of the house

She passed away, I say

Not long after the war, she says

And the house, I say

Sold to pay for the funeral arrangements, that's all, she's buried in Shenandoah, she says

and I nod and the fire cracks and the loons wail and I am tired

It sounds so mournful, she says

It makes that sound to call the other one closer, if they have gotten too far apart, I say

and we sit there without any words between us and this is all we do for a long time, until she sits up straighter in the chair in front of the fire, as if she has remembered a task she has to do and is about to return to it, and I think she might stand up and say good-bye and leave me again, but she draws in a deep breath and goes on with her story, how she stayed with my mother for months and from there tried to get her husband to divorce her, but he would not, because he would have to have paid some amount of alimony, and after my mother died of a cancer that consumed her, Magda moved up to Scranton, where she got a job as a housekeeper in the mansion of a prominent judge and his wife in the Hill Section, and she took care of their three children and became close to the wife, the woman dutiful and alone there in the big house, waiting for something yet to happen to her life, and Magda lived there with them for a long time, the judge even looking into the case of her husband having married her in order to cheat her out of the small fortune her mother had been given by the mining company, extortion, he called it, the full amount of which had been squandered by the man in three short years, and, though there was no restitution, the judge did convince the man to sign divorce papers by having the right people deliver them, he told Magda one day and smiled a rare smile, and in time she forgot the man, poured her life into that family in Scranton, and eventually the children grew and left home and the judge died unexpectedly one night in his bed, and his wife sold the house within the year and moved in with one of her daughters in New York and gave Magda a modest amount of money from what the judge had left her, and she is quiet and I rise to place another birch log on the fire because I have let the fire burn down and I want it burning brightly, and when I sit back down she begins again

And then one day I was shopping at the Boston Store in Wilkes-Barre, where I ran into Nela, Hortensia Holub's daughter, she says and in the firelight she looks both nervous and excited about what she is about to say

Nela insisted we go to lunch at Kresge's, where she told me about her journey here, a journey she called it, that she and her mother had made to see you, the house you live in on a pond in New Hampshire, and how hearing about her father's last moments gave her a peace she had never realized she needed, a difficult peace, but one that brought her and her mother closer as well, she says

I can't imagine they were easy words for Hortensia to hear, I say

They weren't, she says

And so you wanted to make the journey too, I say

No, not right away, I had moved back into our old apartment near the hospital because the landlord's son had taken it over and he remembered us, she says

and her excitement disappears and she seems shy again, reticent almost, and she pushes a few strands of gray hair back behind her ear

I thought being with you when we were younger would have been enough, she says

and she turns to the fire as if an answer were written there, then turns back to me

And then I thought being without you in that place would have helped me see where I went wrong, she says

Where I went wrong, I say

and now I stare into the fire, the brightness of the birch appearing to me as bright as the light of a carbide lamp, and I know what it is she does not see in there, and I tell her that in those days I couldn't bear to close my eyes because I would see their faces and smell their smells and hear the water dripping onto the floor of the mine

And that's what I reminded you of, she says

and it is not a question, in spite of what answer I might give to her

No, in you I saw a glimpse of why God brought me out after your father told me where I would find the way in the last words he uttered, if they were in fact uttered, or somehow spoken to me from beyond that grave, I say

and she breathed in a long deep breath like someone who knew it would not be a long time before she would take her last

I came here, Ondro, because I don't have a lot of time left, so tell me, will you, like you told Nela and Hortensia and the others, she says

and as she waits for me to speak, I have to tell myself that I live far from the patch now, I live in a house on a pond in the shadow of a mountain that will never be mined, and I have worked a long life and it was not a life at work in the mines, and I will live what's left of that life in peace here in this house, and I look at Magda, as old a woman now as I am a man, but a woman whom I have loved since she was a girl and who was once my wife, and though she is backlit by the fire in the fireplace like some spirit who is haunted by a secret left unknown in the living world, she is no ghost, no, she is flesh and blood and she is in my home, and so I begin, and I tell her about that January morning I went down in the mines for the first time as a mule boy, the cold and the line and the cage and the miners and their butties and what they spoke of and what her father said to me, and then the work and the satisfaction, yes, that I was doing what I was good at doing, and the mule, Wicked, and the Šariš Slovak I spoke to him, and the skill and speed with which that beast and I both worked, and I pause for a moment before I tell her what admiration I remember having for her father, even after all these years, how he worked, the way he worked, how beautiful it was to watch a man like him at work, and then I tell her what I can about the explosion and the collapse, just as I had told the others, and I tell her about the deaths of the butties Matty and Emil and, in time, the death of Štefan Bozak, all of which I had told the others who came to me, all of which I had told my friend Jacobson in prison long before that, but it finally occurs to me there before the fire in the evening of the late summer that I had never told any of this to Magda, not when we were children, or when we were at college and I was taking the bus back and forth between Wilkes-Barre and the Back Mountain, or when we were silent and lying next to each other in our most intimate moments as husband and wife, I never told her about her father, John Chibala, the last one to speak to me in the mines, never told her even of the fear I felt in those days I was trapped underground with him, my fear of being alone and how he did what he could to assuage that for me, a boy of thirteen wondering if this would become his grave, I couldn't tell her about her father, because I needed to leave my fear behind and believed that saying nothing about it was the only way, leave it in the dark, leave it where no one created by God would ever set eyes on those men again, even when it was as much a part of me as my own eyes and ears and hands, and I don't know if I should go on telling her tonight, because I am still afraid

You've lost too much to gain so little of my telling it to you now, I say

and she is still backlit by the fire, which is burning down because we have been talking, and that birch is the last log I placed on the flames

It's all loss in the end, Ondro, so tell me, tell me because we're both close to the end, and I want to hear it, she says

and I stand and take an oak log from the log rack and place it on the fire and sit down and wait and watch as it catches slowly at the corners, then begins to burn, and I tell her that after Štefan Bozak died

I collected the carbides he had collected from the butties Matty and Emil and put them in my coat pocket and took the lamp from Štefan Bozak's hat and whispered there in the dark that I was sorry to steal from him, but I was taking the light so I could find a way out of there for all of us, and I cleaned the burner tip and filled the bottom with carbides and the tank with water from the growler that was collecting ceiling drip and fixed the lamp on John Chibala's head because his lamp was clogged with dust and wouldn't light anymore, and I rolled the flint lighter and the lamp flared bright and white and lit up the small room, and John Chibala looked up and focused the lamp on the rock pile that had sealed us in

That's where you want to dig, Ondro, he said

and I turned to the pile and began moving rock and slate and slabs of anthracite until my hands were cut raw, and still we found no place where we could detect air or light or any other sign that a shaft might be out there somewhere, or searchers in search of us out there, and I stopped after what might have been an hour and John Chibala turned down his light and told me to do the same with mine, and we sat in the darkness again and drank from the pail that had already collected more water dripping from the ceiling of the room

Could he move at all, could he even have walked if you had found a way out, she says

His legs were pinned under rock and his back was probably broken in the collapse, I say

and she turns to the fire, stares at the light, then brushes her cheek with her sleeve and turns back to me again

He believed in you, she says

and Magda Chibala falls silent and lowers her head, and I let her sit in her silence and the distance of the years in which we both knew the patch and the colliery and our mothers and the men who left our houses there and, with the help of God, came back each day, until the day they could not, not would not but could not, that day not so far from us in our memories, even now that we are both old

I've always wondered about his last moments in the dark, and you with him, she says

The memento mori, Jacobson called it, I say

Yes, Sister Bernadette once said the same to me, when she asked how my father died and I told her it was in a mine collapse, that I should find peace knowing he wasn't killed in the moment, because he was given the gift of understanding and accepting the moment of his death, she says

I don't know that it was a gift, I say

and she looks away and wipes her cheeks with her hand again, and I remember that, but for the fire, we are in the dark

If I could go back to the days before we were married when we sat in that café down the hill from the college and drank coffee, that's what I would ask, what I wanted to ask but didn't know then how to ask, she says

and we sit and listen to the low breath sound of fire consuming the oak log, the breeze that pushes against the window screen from outside, and the ghostly echo on that breeze of the loon in search of its mate farther out on the pond

We were so young, and I didn't know how, she says

and I wish and don't wish now that we were back in the café in Dallas, Pennsylvania

And yet, that was the question that sat at the back of my mind, like an old woman waiting for the chance to speak of what she always knew she wanted to ask the man who watched her father die, she says

The others died quickly, I say

and we are both staring into the fire as I speak

But your father had a will to him, even crushed under rock, as though everything we did had a place, everything part of something seen or unseen, as long as we did what was next, I say

and I tell her that even the butties Matty and Emil, who said little and died first, understood their moments of death, understood the moment as a moment of life as alive as the one before it, and on their lips were those who loved them, whom they loved even more, the ones who, in their time, came to me to hear the same, and perhaps that's what those last gasps and whispers and professions of love were meant for, like Štefan Bozak's knowing that his children knew their father loved them, but in the end it was John Chibala and I who sat in the dark, and I was only thirteen and terrified and believing that I too would die in the dark, and he never cried out in what must have been blinding pain, and he told me not to worry, he always said, Ondro, ňestaraj śe, and asked me in the end what I was afraid of, if it was fear that was overtaking me, and I told him I was afraid of being alone down there, still alive, and all of the others dead, and he said, Yes, that is something to fear, but if you are alive, alone or with others, in the dark or in the light, imprisoned or walking freely, it is life right up to the last breath, and I asked him if he thought it would be painful, and he said, It's painful now, and tried to laugh, and then said, You're too young to have traveled anywhere, but many of us in the patch have left entire countries and lives to come here to work, your father one of them, and the hardest thing for us was to let those lives slip over the horizon like the last time a sun will ever set, never to be seen again, and that pain is like a wound long and deep that takes a long time to heal, but it heals, it's just that the missing becomes a part of living every day, and then we didn't talk for a long time, and I listened to the water from the ceiling dripping into the pail and thought he had fallen asleep, or maybe died already, until he said, Yes, we miss them every day, and so I asked him whom he would miss the most, and he said without a moment of hesitation, I'll miss my Magda the most, miss seeing her when I come home in the evening and in the mornings on the days I don't work, and I'll miss seeing her grow into a young woman, will miss knowing what and whom she has become as a young woman, whom she will love, and where that will be, away from here, I hope, but not too far away, because I will want to see her always, but away from here, and then we were both silent again, for longer than I can say because I think I had fallen asleep, yes, I know now that we had both fallen asleep, for how long I don't know, but all of a sudden I woke up in the pitch-black to a smell that was getting stronger and more foul, something rotting, something I had never smelled before in my life in the small room where the miners John Chibala and Štefan Bozak, and their butties Matty and Emil were trapped, and still I believed it was John Chibala who heard me stir

You smell that too, don't you, Ondro

and I heard what I thought was John Chibala's voice and sat up and took a deep breath and was sorry I did and was about to ask if it was Matty and Emil, whose bodies lay close to us

No, Ondro, that's the mule, Wicked, he's under the rock, that's where it's coming from

It's already been days then, hasn't it, I said

It's been more than four days

Will they still be looking for us, I said

Not for much longer, there's only one way out for you now

and it was a risk but the only one I knew that could work, and perhaps it was meant to work all along, the mule himself having seen to it, but I couldn't know until I could smell him

You can't crawl through rock, Ondro, but you can crawl through rotting mule

and I was certain it was John Chibala's voice, but when I rose and lit my lamp the man's eyes were closed and his face was as silent and bloodless white as the rest of the men in that room, but I knew, I knew, and I lit the lamp attached to the peak of his hat and touched his eyes closed and shined my lamp on the place where I stood when the collapse had occurred, the place Wicked the mule lay buried under stone, the place from which the stench of rotting flesh had begun to rise, and I began to dig, to move away rock and slate and slabs of scree and anthracite, and the smell got stronger and stronger, until it repulsed me and yet drew me toward it, and I pulled harder and faster at the rocks, breathing deeper and getting closer to the source of that stench, then I touched it, the soft flesh of Wicked's eye, I knew, because my hand and fingers had grazed the forehead of the beast as I reached in to pull away yet another slab and found the softness of the eye socket and my finger sank in, and I pulled it out and felt the jelly of the eye and held up my hand to look at it in the light of the lamp

Yes, it's there, the way out is there

and I wiped my hand and fingers dripping with eye on my thin coat, and pulled more rock away from where I could see by my lamp Wicked was positioned, his back bracing up a huge slab of coal from that last pillar, sheer black and flat and running along the length of the mule, and right at the place where the spine met the flat of that slab there was a small area in the shape of an upside-down vee, and that was where I would crawl, and I got down on my hands and knees and looked through that space of the upside-down vee, the light from my lamp bouncing off the shiny black diamond side of the slab and along the length of it, and I could see something flitting back and forth, no, not something, some things, rats, running back and forth, and then, in the light, a glint of the steel rail along which the cars I had jockeyed as a spragger ran, and I raised my head and turned to John Chibala and shined my lamp like a sun on his face, his eyes closed still, as if he were asleep, and no longer any trace of pain on his face

I will be back for you and the others, I said

and I turned and knelt down again and let my body drop to the ground and took a deep breath and held it and began to shimmy along that ground, along the rotting back of Wicked the mule with the sheer flat face of a slab of coal hard against my own back, and the hair and skin of the mule came off the beast and hung up in the carbide lamp as I squeezed past and snuffed out the light before I was even halfway through, the smell so suffocating I thought of turning around, but another part of me thought of the others and believed that I might be able to get men down there to clear the rock and bring them out, and I could hear ňestaraj śe in a voice like a whisper, and so I ignored my fear and crawled forward, the passageway getting smaller, the upside-down vee getting narrower, my only hope the path pushing farther along the rotting flesh of the mule, until my arms and hands out in front of me were pulling the skin and fur off the beast as I clawed through the dark toward the end of the passage, toward the end, so that my final push was into the putrid haunches of Wicked the mule, the same animal that saved my life, and I pushed and pulled at his ass and thighs, until my head emerged into the tunnel where I could hear thousands of rats squeaking and gnawing at the dead and decomposing animal's hooves and legs and back on the other side of the rock, and they crawled over me and bit at me as I kept crawling in the dark toward where I knew the rail would be, the rail along which I had brought so many cars loaded with the coal the miners John Chibala and Štefan Bozak and their butties Matty and Emil had brought out of breast number seven, days and days before, and I pulled the last of my body from the carcass of Wicked and stood and threw off my hat and the lamp in the direction of those rats and heard it clank along the stone floor before they smothered it, then I knelt down again and touched the rail and began crawling along that steel strand, yard after yard, the darkness all too familiar to me, as though I would not have known what to do if I had somehow emerged from that room into light, until I came to a ventilation door that had been blocked by some falling rocks, no doubt from what had brought down breast number seven, and I was overcome with a rage that, after all these days, days in which I could do nothing but watch men die, I would still be trapped in that mine, and I pushed and pushed at the door in my rage, pushed until it opened just enough for me to slide past, though it peeled back my coat and scraped skin off my chest and I could hear ribs crack as I worked my way through, but when I emerged I could see in the distance along the tracks a trace of light from some electrical lamps that had been strung along a main shaft, and it was still far away, but it was a point I could focus on, and I stood up then and began to walk between the rails, not stumbling or running, walking steadily, all of my muscles and each one of my bones groaning and aching within me, and the light began to grow and grow, and I could hear voices then, voices of men calling out directions, the light from their own carbides sweeping across the walls of those shafts until I was face-to-face with one of those men, and we stopped and looked at each other and he whispered, My God, My God, then turned and began hollering so loudly it was deafening to me there in that mine shaft, and I collapsed and don't remember being carried through those shafts to the escape tunnel, and I don't remember the conversations the other men who came with a stretcher had with each other and tried to have with me about where they could find the miners John Chibala and Štefan Bozak and their butties Matty and Emil, until they leaned close in and winced from the smell of death on my face and asked, Are they alive, son, and I shook my head, and they asked, Where, and I said, The smell, and they didn't ask me again, they ran as fast as they could along the tracks in the direction of the collapse, the lamps at the peaks of their caps bouncing light along those walls like a train of mules set loose and running wildly, and I was blinded by the daylight when I came up and out of the shaft and the door opened and Ruka was there, and he picked me up off the stretcher and carried me over to someone standing at the edge of the crowd and placed me in a blanket on the ground, and I saw the outline of my mother standing in front of me like an angel blocking out the light, or a ghost, I couldn't tell, but she reached down to embrace me and held me and I could hear her sobbing, everyone and everything else around me quiet, not even the breaker humming, and then someone asked about the other four, the miners and their butties, and I heard a voice say, No, it's only the mule boy, and then the chorus of wailing

VIII

AND ON THIS MORNING HE WALKS DOWN THE DIRT path from the house to the pond, stepping between thick white pine roots that stretch across the path like ranges across a continent and past blueberry bushes that in the summer are bent and weighed down by their plentiful and ripened fruit, but bear only green leaves now, and the dawn light through the yellow leaves of the beech and birch has brightened beyond the gray of first light before the sun breaks the horizon of the hill to the east and rises above the pond and shines out over thc water like some benevolent and exploding star that is marveled at, not feared, from a distance, shines like it does every morning he wakes to sun, shining even in the dead of winter on ice and snow so blue it looks a painted sky altogether, and he sees her from the distance of the path, sees her sitting by the water in one of the two chairs he built from the red oak he and the sawyer had cut down and cured and milled into planks then measured and fashioned into the backs and sides and seats he fastened together, chairs that sit out all summer at the water's edge, and her body is wrapped in a blanket for warmth against the morning chill that begins to descend in August and is considerable this fall, but she has been up early this morning, as she is every morning, coming down to the pondside to sit before the sun rises, to listen to the mournful wailing of the loons, and to wait for him, as she has waited all her life, and he remembers the picnic when he was a boy and his father was still alive and they had left the patch to go into town, where there was a park and picnic tables and grass, and all of the miners and the butties and their families looked changed there in a place that was not their home, and he saw a young girl in the distance, her black hair unloosened and wild-looking, her eyes gray and serene, and he asked his father who she was and he told his son it was the miner John Chibala's daughter and that the man loved her very much because she was the only child he could have, and he wondered what his father meant by that because he knew his mother was expecting another child, another brother or sister to him, though her belly was not yet big, and all the miners and their butties seemed to have more children than one could count sometimes, and he looked at the girl and her wild black hair and gray eyes and walked over to her, and she looked up and said, My name is Magda, would you like to sit with me, and he did, and they sat like that all day, he not saying much of anything to her, only answering her questions out of a boy's shyness and the fear she might leave him if he spoke too much, and then the families ate and the children played and the day was over, and not long afterward his father died when the mine breast in which he was working collapsed, and it was a long time before he spoke to or even looked at Magda Chibala again, but on this day he stops for a moment in the path of the big white pine roots and blueberry bushes and listens to a loon call, watches its mate dive out on the pond before him, and he fingers the old wooden rosary in his pocket, the one that hasn't left him, except for his time in prison, for the three-quarters of a century since his mother had given it to him for his birthday after his father died, more than a century since it had been carved from the limb of a tree that was all his father had brought from the old country, and he thinks he should try to say an Ave Maria, but he doesn't remember the words anymore, then thinks it's not the prayer or the sound of the prayer but the feel of the wood that changes him, and he reaches into the pocket where he keeps the old rosary this morning and every morning, and touches his father and his mother and the woman Magda Chibala, who loved him the day she held the beads long enough for them to receive her, and his prayer is that she will love him again, and this is prayer enough, if prayer were ever more than a summoning, a waiting, a place to hope, because it's all he has left of any prayer he once remembered, and he lets go of the old rosary in his pocket and reaches for the collar on his coat and turns it up against the wind coming off the pond, he feeling the cold a little sharper now too in his old age, and goes to her, the woman sitting down by the pond, the woman he waited for, and now she for him on an autumn morning, and it is all one to them, this time they have left, where they are to begin, there they will return again

Acknowledgments

Lines cited from the writings of Moses Maimonides are taken from *The Guide of the Perplexed*, volume I, translated and with an introduction and notes by Shlomo Pines (University of Chicago Press, 1963). Lines cited from the writings of Parmenides of Elea are taken from *Fragments: A Text and Translation with an Introduction*, translated by David Gallop (University of Toronto Press, 1984). Lines cited from the text of the Book of Jonah are taken from *The Hebrew Bible: A Translation with Commentary*, volume 2, *Prophets: Nevi'im*, by Robert Alter (W. W. Norton, 2019). I am grateful to Rabbi Annie Fantasia for her help and direction getting started reading and writing Hebrew, and to Kyra Siegel for catching my mistakes. I would also like to thank the following for their collective help with the Šariš dialect of Slovak: Prof. Katarína Balleková, Prof. Jozef Bilsky, Prof. Adriana Ferencikova, Prof. Renata Kamenárová, and Prof. Gabriela Mucskova. The following early readers of *Mule Boy* gave me invaluable feedback: Jared Crawford, Anthony Domestico, Amelia Dunlop, Royal Hansen, Larry Seidl, and Josh Weil. Also, I want to thank the staff at Bellevue Literary Press: Carol Edwards, Joe Gannon, Laura Hart, and Elana Rosenthal, who make sure books are as fine and beautiful as they can be; Molly Mikolowski, who is tireless in her desire to get those books out into the world; and Erika Goldman, without whom there wouldn't be any books. And finally, I am grateful to my aunt Genevieve Harenza for her willingness to share memories of the stories her mother told her about the Pennsylvania coal mines before the Second World War, and the men who died in them, including the father she never met but whom she knew her entire life.

The publication of this book is made possible by the support of Jerome and Lois Lowenstein.

Bellevue Literary Press is devoted to publishing literary fiction and nonfiction at the intersection of the arts and sciences because we believe that science and the humanities are natural companions for understanding the human experience. We feature exceptional literature that explores the nature of consciousness, embodiment, and the underpinnings of the social contract. With each book we publish, our goal is to foster a rich, interdisciplinary dialogue that will forge new tools for thinking and engaging with the world.

To support our press and its mission, and for our full catalogue of published titles, please visit us at blpress.org.

Bellevue Literary Press
New York